JUST CHILL

ALSO AVAILABLE:

BY **ANDY MCGUIRE**
ILLUSTRATIONS BY **GIRISH MANUEL**

PRESS

Copyright ©2024 by Minno Press
Published in association with Minno Kids®

Cover copyright ©2024 by Minno Press

Minno Press and Minno Kids® are divisions of Winsome Truth, Inc.

Minno Press
818 18th Ave South
10th Floor
Nashville, TN 37203
gominno.com/press

Micah's Super Vlog was created by Girish Manuel. Micah's Super Vlog trademark and character rights are owned by Square One World Media, Inc., and used by permission.

Written by Andy McGuire
Illustrated by Girish Manuel and Stu Hunnable

First Edition: October 2019

Library of Congress Cataloging-in-Publication Data has been applied for.

ISBN: 978-1-5460-2659-4

Printed in the USA.

To my wife, Becky, for always being ready to laugh with me,
at me, or near me, depending on what the situation calls for.

—AM

To my parents, thank you for always
pushing me to do more and be more.

—GM

CHAPTER ONE

"The throne is mine, and there is nothing you can do to stop me!" growls the evil hunchback.

"Help! Helo! The hunchback has kidnapped me!" screams Princess Eleandor. As she sees the hero approaching, she shouts with sigh-filled victory, "Helo! My hero!"

"It's the end of the line, evildoer! I, the mighty Helo, will save Princess Eleandor from your clutches! There's nowhere to run!" exclaims Helo as he swings his mighty sword. "Take that! And that!" he shouts. But every swing Helo takes is deflected, dodged, and countered.

"How is it that you know my every move?!" Helo questions. "You're but a mere peasant hunchback . . . You couldn't possibly have been trained in the art of sword fighting."

"Mwah-ha-ha-ha!" the hunchback laughs evilly. "Perhaps you and I aren't so different, Helo."

"Enough of your games! What do you speak of?" Helo looks confused.

"You still don't recognize me? Behold . . ." The hunchback removes his hood. "I am your long-lost twin brother, Url!"

"Impossible!" Helo says, stunned. "My twin brother has been long lost!"

"That's what I said!" Url replies.

"But Url! Why have you turned to evil?" Helo asks, still confused.

"Not sure, really. How's Mom doing, by the way? Is she making meatballs for supper?" Url asks.

Eleandor taps her foot and huffs.

"Cut!" Micah Murphy yelled as he walked over

to his friends with the confidence of a fifth-grade moviemaker.

"Gabe, why would Url want to come over for dinner?! He's in the middle of capturing the princess! And can we stay in character next time? And Gabe, I want to hear more hunchback growl and less angry kid in your delivery. Lydia, Eleandor is sure Helo will save her. I want to feel that confidence when you deliver your lines."

Wow! He sounded like a real director, and it felt great! Micah was just about to drift off into one of his regular daydreams, complete with stage lighting, multiple cameras, and a director's chair, when the bell rang.

Recess was over. His dream would have to wait.

"The first day after Christmas break is clearly the worst day of the year," Micah said as he and his friends shuffled back to the classroom.

"Are you kidding me?" Lydia asked. "It doesn't even compare to the first day after summer vacation.

At least with the day after Christmas break we're already halfway done with the school year!"

"That's ridiculous," Micah challenged. "The first day after summer vacation isn't so bad. Everybody knows you don't do any real work until the second week of school. On week one the teachers spend all their time learning names and making seating charts and then figuring out that none of the kids go by their real names anyway, and then learning their nicknames and throwing away the seating charts and doing it all over again. It's awesome!"

Lydia shrugged and nodded. Micah had never seen her give up on an argument so quickly. "Good point," she conceded. "There's definitely something about the first day after Christmas break that makes the blood run cold. Nobody's in the mood to learn, but the teachers don't care—they get right into their assignments anyway."

"Yeah," Armin said, glaring at the open history book in front of him. "We need something to make life interesting again, like it was back during Christmas break."

"You mean yesterday?" Lydia asked.

Armin nodded. "Exactly!"

Micah agreed, but thankfully, he had his movie on his mind, and recess had been the perfect chance to rehearse. But now, it was time to get back to reality.

It was only five minutes later that Micah's friends got exactly what they wanted—something new and interesting. Mr. Drury, the principal of New Leaf Elementary, told Micah's teacher over the intercom that he'd be stopping by. He was going to bring their fifth-grade class a new student.

Suddenly Micah wasn't thinking about his movie anymore, and he especially couldn't focus on their history chapter. How could he possibly care about cotton gins (whatever those were) when a new kid was about to shake things up? Granted, Micah wasn't one to care about cotton gins under the best of circumstances, but now he *really* couldn't concentrate. As he glanced around the room, everyone else seemed to be in the same boat. Gins, cotton or otherwise, didn't stand a chance.

Poor Mr. Turtell, Micah's teacher, tried to quickly tidy himself up before the principal arrived. He straightened his tie, made sure the back of his shirt was tucked in, and felt around in his pockets for something.

"Has anyone seen my mustache comb?" he asked the classroom.

"What's a mustache comb?" Micah whispered to Lydia.

Lydia looked at him quizzically. "Well, piecing together the context clues, it's most likely a comb used for mustaches."

"Oh yeah. That makes sense."

The door opened, and Mr. Drury walked in.

"May I have your attention?" he asked. It was a completely unnecessary question. Every eye was already on him, and the boy was by his side. "I'd like to introduce you to Tre Buzznik, the newest member

of your class. Tre just moved here from California and doesn't know anyone at New Leaf Elementary. So please try to be friendly."

He started to walk out the door, but then paused. "Or at least not mean. Or scary. Or weird."

At New Leaf Elementary, all those warnings were necessary. This was a school that had a reputation for making new kids call home to mommy before lunch. But as Mr. Drury left Tre to fend for himself in Mr. Turtell's class, Micah could tell something was different about this kid. All around he could hear awed whispers as his classmates looked him up and down.

"Is he cool?" asked Eric. "He looks cool."

"His jacket sure is," said Armin. "It's a Swish brand! They're so expensive, my mom said I could either get a Swish jacket or go to college."

"I'd choose the jacket," said Liam, staring at Tre in awe.

"I hope he hangs out with me," said Gabe. "Then I can be cool too!"

"Nobody's cool enough to make *you* cool," said Makayla. "But I sure do like the way he walks. It's, like, this casual strut."

"But without looking like he's trying too hard," added Mara. "And check out his skateboard! I can tell he's awesome at it just by looking at him."

"And I can tell zat he is rich," said Hanz. "Rich people like us can spot each uzzer from many miles away."

"I hope he's a nerd," said Chet. "Rich nerds are great for bullying!"

"That's no nerd smile," said Katie. "Look at those dimples!"

Lydia nodded. "Not to mention that hair! A nerd could never pull that look off."

"What's the big deal?" asked Micah to no one in particular. He was annoyed. He wasn't exactly sure what he was annoyed by, but he felt like someone should object to what was happening. Everyone ignored him.

"Did you see how his hair bounces when he

tosses his head to the side?" asked Makayla. "I could totally die!"

But there was no more time to analyze the way he looked, because now it was time to analyze the way he talked.

"Class," said Mr. Turtell, "let's all listen to Tre as he tells us a little about himself. Tre, please tell us where you're from and anything else you'd like us to know."

Tre looked around the room, flipped his hair out of his eyes, and smiled. It was like a shampoo commercial, a designer clothes commercial, and a toothpaste commercial all rolled into one!

"Yo. As you heard, I'm Tre. My last school was in San Diego, and before that I lived in LA, spending my time hanging at the beach, surfin' waves, or riding my board in the neighborhood. I loved Cali, but I'm happy to be here in Middletown, hanging with ya. I hope we can all be friends."

Interesting, Micah thought to himself. His voice was even cooler than his looks! How was that possible? Tre had a super chill, California accent that even made the name Middletown sound cool when he said it. And everyone knew there was nothing cool about Middletown.

Things I've Learned That Fifth-Grade Boys Should Have If They Want Girls to Think They're Cool

- Good hygiene: shower now and then

- Confidence: Occasionally try to make eye contact

- A good smell: don't cover up old sneaker stink with spray-on deodorant

- Great hair: the floppier the better

- An accent: it's always better to sound like you're from somewhere else

- Nice clothes: clean and appropriate (try to avoid video game–themed T-shirts at weddings and funerals)

- Table manners: Don't ask girls if they like seafood, then show them half-eaten food in your mouth (they don't think this is funny)

- Proper pronunciation: Always remember to pronounce the first "r" in "library" (but for some reason it's not as important to pronounce the first "r" in "February" . . . go figure)

As Tre sat down, the whispering around the room continued.

"Definitely cool," said Eric.

Chet shrugged and nodded. "Yeah. He's probably too cool for me to bully. That's disappointing."

"He lived in San Diego? And LA?" said Katie. "I might just faint right here!"

"And his accent is *amazing*!" Makayla sighed. "Every word he says is like a vacation to my ears!"

Lydia nodded in wide-eyed agreement. "I can almost feel the sun on my face and the sand between my toes!"

"Seriously, I could listen to him talk all day," said Katie.

"His whole . . . vibe," said Makayla. "There's only one word for it . . ."

Katie, Makayla, and Lydia exchanged glances.

"Dreamy!" they all said at exactly the same time. Then they giggled like it was the funniest joke they had ever heard.

"Oh, come on, guys. The way he talks is nothing special," said Micah, doing his best to slow down his voice and fake a cool California accent of his own. "Anyone can, like, speak that way. It's totally not that hard, dude."

Armin gave him a funny look. "You okay? Your voice is all deep and slow."

"Is something wrong with your tongue?" Liam asked.

"Did you go to the dentist this morning?" Gabe joined in. "After they fixed my last cavity, I couldn't pronounce the letter *R* for a week!"

"Wow!" said Armin. "That's a long time. Is that what's wrong with you, Micah?"

Micah sighed. "No. I was just . . . Never mind."

The class was still buzzing with energy when Mr. Turtell had to drop them off at music class. Micah didn't have a good feeling about this. His classmates were hard to control in music class anyway. Add in the excitement of a new kid, and who knew what could happen?

Mrs. Huang, the music teacher, passed out instruments to the classroom. There was a wood block, a cowbell, a couple of tambourines, three recorders, a xylophone, and a triangle.

"I hope you all had a wonderful Christmas break! I know you haven't been in class with me for almost three weeks, but I'm sure you still remember the parts I taught you to 'Go Tell Aunt Rhodie'!"

Micah felt sorry for Mrs. Huang. She always started each lesson with such joy and enthusiasm, but by the end the kids always left her in confusion and despair.

"Okay, from the top," Mrs. Huang announced. "Get your instruments ready. And sing loud and clear! Don't be afraid to be heard. One, two, ready, go!"

And then there was chaos.

Picture half a dozen angry chimpanzees banging on pots and pans in a small kitchen. Now imagine tossing a handful of tone-deaf hyenas into the mix, who seem to believe the best way to fix wrong notes is by singing them louder. Then throw in a flock of squealing cockatoos to hit all the high parts. Of a completely different song.

Whatever you're imagining, you're not even close. It was so much worse than that.

"Cut! Cut!" Mrs. Huang shouted. "I think we need to take it slowly. Back to the very beginning. Gabe, please play the first few notes of "Go Tell Aunt Rhodie" for us on your xylophone."

But Gabe wasn't paying attention.

"I think his fingers are stuck in the keys again," said Makayla helpfully.

Mrs. Huang sighed. "Could you help him with that, Makayla? And then trade him your recorder for his xylophone?"

"I'd be glad to sing the first few lines to get us going," offered Chet.

The whole class stared at him in surprise.

"Thank you, Chet. That would be great," said Mrs. Huang, a look of proud pleasure on her face—the look of a teacher who's finally gotten through to a difficult student.

Chet took a deep breath and sang to the rafters:

"Go tell Aunt Rhodie
She's a weird old fogey.
Who smells like a hoagie
And probably wets the bed."

His lyrics rarely made sense, but Micah had to admit he had a good sense for rhyme. Mrs. Huang seemed unimpressed. She held her head in her hands and took a deep breath.

"What zis song needs is ze glockenspiel!" Hanz said. "Zat is a beautiful instrument—ze instrument of my people!"

"I don't think that would fix the problem," said Lydia.

"You don't know zat it wouldn't!" said Hanz.

"Okay!" Mrs. Huang shouted, then regained her composure. "Let's start from the top once again. Makayla, could you play the first few notes for us, please?"

She did.

And then everyone joined in.

More chaos.

Chimpanzees banged. Hyenas howled. Cockatoos shrieked. Mr. Drury even peeked his head in for a moment to make sure no one was in pain. Seeing that they weren't, he ducked back out again and hurried away from the noise.

But then, out of nowhere, something surprising happened.

Micah couldn't put his finger on what it was at first, but there seemed to be a brand-new sound piercing through the racket. And the weird thing was, it actually sounded *good*! Almost like someone was hitting notes that were supposed to be hit. Even the rhythm seemed . . . rhythmic.

It was all very confusing, and no one knew what to do at first. Then, one by one, everyone stopped the bad noises they were making to listen to the good one.

Little by little the room grew quieter and quieter, until finally there was only a single voice, ringing out soft but clear. It was Tre's.

"Go tell Aunt Rhodie
Go tell Aunt Rhodie
Go tell Aunt Rhodie
The old gray goose is dead."

Micah had never heard anything so beautiful in his life. He looked around the room. Everyone was staring at Tre, mouths half-open in wonder.

In the silence they could hear kindergartners in the classroom next door.

Several of them were weeping.

"Why, Mrs. Harper?" one of them asked. "Why did the old gray goose have to die?"

Micah heard a sniffle beside him. He looked over at Chet, who was wiping an eye.

"Hay fever," Chet said quietly, under his breath.

Mrs. Huang smiled. "Well, now I think we're getting somewhere!"

"That was awesome," said Lydia.

"Incredible," said Eric.

"Amazing," said Katie.

"Rururrah," said Gabe.

"What was that?" asked Mrs. Huang.

Makayla shook her head and sighed. "Now Gabe's lip is stuck in the recorder."

The New Kid

Of all the horrible things that could happen on the already horrible first day after Christmas break . . . a new kid?! Things have been going well around here lately. My friends are awesome, and we've got this epic movie to make. We don't need a new guy in school to mess it all up.

Lydia thinks he's "dreamy" (at least I think that's what she and the other girls said) . . . whatever that means. I mean, what's so special about him? Big deal . . . he talks cool, walks cool, has cool hair . . . You know what's worse?! He can sing.

Nope. We do not need a dreamy, talented new guy at New Leaf Elementary. I just need to make sure I (and my friends) can steer clear of him. We don't have room for any more friends in our group. I'm sure Armin and Lydia would agree.

A heart at peace gives life to the body, but envy rots the bones.
Proverbs 14:30 (NIV)

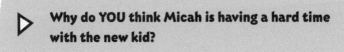

▷ **Have YOU ever had a new kid in your class? How did it make you feel?**

▷ **Why do YOU think Micah is having a hard time with the new kid?**

CHAPTER TWO

Today was a rare day for New Leaf Elementary fifth graders. Today Micah and his friends would get to enjoy second recess—a small incentive for dealing with the pain of returning to school after Christmas break!

Micah hurried from the lunchroom to his bonus recess with a belly full of tater tots and a head full of big ideas. He, Armin, and Lydia would continue working on the script of his epic fantasy movie. They were almost ready to start filming! Micah was the director and cameraman, and Lydia and Armin were the big stars. Gabe; Micah's sister, Audrey; and Micah's dog, Barnabas, were the supporting cast. It

was a long shot, but Micah was hoping they could even get it into the upcoming Middletown film festival!

Micah tried to ignore the smooth-talking, perfectly coiffed elephant on the playground (aka the new kid) as he looked around for a place to work on his script. Tre was sitting alone by the teachers. All of a sudden Micah felt that maybe he should go over and introduce himself, but he didn't have time for that.

They just had a few more details to hammer out before letting the cameras roll. Micah, Lydia, Armin, and Gabe found a spot under a tree out of the way and tried to ignore the recess madness as it swirled around them.

"Remind me what my character's motivation is again," Armin said to Micah. "Does he have some sort of backstory that's made him who he is?"

"Helo is a proud and lonesome warrior who's been beaten down by life."

"I'm with you so far," said Armin. "But how, exactly, has he been beaten down?"

Micah hadn't worked out all the backstory details yet. Or any of them, really. But he didn't want to admit it. "Well . . . um . . . I think it was mostly that . . . um . . . he always wanted a dog, but his mom was more of a cat person."

He was on a roll now, so he figured he'd just keep it going. "And then one day he finally grew up and moved out on his own, so, of course, he got a dog. He named it . . . um . . . Sparky."

"Okay . . . ," said Armin.

"But then he lost him. You can only imagine the heartbreak! He started wandering in the wilderness on his own, sleeping under the stars and looking for Sparky, only to discover that he hated campfire meals and was totally scared of the dark!"

"Scared of the dark?" asked Armin. "Really?"

"Yeah," said Micah. "Helo has to come to terms with who he is. He has to accept himself—the good and the bad—and not pretend he's somebody he's not or compare himself to other people."

"Of course!" said Lydia. "That's brilliant! Every hero needs a weakness. It makes them relatable and stuff. Okay, now what's my backstory?"

"Well," said Micah, "as you know, you're a dethroned elf queen."

"How was I dethroned? I thought I was super strong and powerful."

"You are, but . . . um . . . your hair is your source of power. And you didn't even know it! And then one day you had to cut it, so you lost your power."

"But why did I have to cut my hair?"

"Because . . ." Micah paused, trying to come up with something brilliant. "You got gum in it!"

"Okay," said Lydia. "That makes sense. So, when my hair grows back, I'll be strong again?"

"Exactly!" said Micah. "You have to bide your time until then. But even when you're not strong, you're still really smart, but also a little bossy."

"Bossy?" said Lydia, glaring at Micah. "I don't know if I'm comfortable with that."

"Every hero needs a weakness," Armin quipped with a smirk.

Micah ignored them. "And Gabe, remember: you're the evil hunchback who's currently on the throne, trying to keep the elf princess from regaining power. You've always wanted the power she's had, and the jealousy has consumed you!"

Gabe gave him a thumbs-up. "Got it. Evil hunchback."

Micah looked back over at Lydia, but she wasn't paying attention to him anymore. She was staring at Tre, carrying his skateboard as he walked from group to group. "Look at him, wandering around recess, trying to find his place in the crowd."

"Looks like the soccer kids are asking if he wants to join them," said Armin. "He's probably telling them he just wants to get the lay of the land today."

Lydia nodded. "Now it looks like he's politely declining the card players, the tag players, and the basketball players. Undoubtedly with a gracious 'thank you' and a smile, of course."

"Wow. Everyone wants him to be part of their group!" Micah said with a bit of sarcasm in his voice. Or was that jealousy?

"It makes sense," Armin said. "He seems like a really nice guy."

"He hasn't even been here a day and he's already so popular." Micah had meant to keep this thought to himself, but it was out before he knew it.

Lydia looked at him strangely. "What's that supposed to mean?"

"It's just . . . ," Micah started. But there was no backing down now. "Why is he already so popular? What is it about him?" Micah couldn't put his finger on it. "Maybe it's his hair? Or his chill accent? He can't really be this perfect."

"There's nothing wrong with being perfect," said Lydia, staring at Tre and grinning from ear to ear.

Armin shook his head. "I think you're crazy, Micah."

"Totally crazy," said Lydia.

"I'm not crazy. *You're* crazy!" Micah shouted.

"Who's crazy?" said someone with a chill, California accent. Micah turned around to see Tre right behind him. He must have been slowly making his way over to their spot under the tree while Micah was busy losing his mind.

"Um . . . Gabe's crazy, of course," Micah answered. He felt like an idiot and wanted to get the attention off himself. Luckily, Gabe was being . . . Gabe. Which meant he was a prime candidate to be accused of craziness. At the moment he was thirty feet away, lying flat on his belly with his arms at his sides, moaning in a deep voice.

"What, exactly, is that dude doing?" Tre asked.

"No idea," said Micah. He turned to Gabe and shouted, "Gabe, what are you doing?"

"Getting into character," Gabe answered. Then he looked over at Tre. "I'm a hunchback whale!"

Lydia sighed. She didn't bother to correct him.

"We're making a movie," Armin said to Tre.

For some reason Micah found himself not wanting Tre to know about their movie. But it was too late now.

"Gabe's playing an evil hunchback," said Lydia. "Apparently he thought he was playing an evil humpback."

Tre nodded, as if it all made sense now. "That's cool. I'm Tre, by the way. I was introduced to the whole class, but I haven't, like, met everyone yet."

"I'm Lydia."

"I'm Armin."

"I'm Micah."

"How about you show us some tricks on that thing?" Armin said, pointing to Tre's skateboard.

"Nah. This rocky ground would totally wreck my wheels."

They didn't know where to go from there, so they surveyed the rest of the recess scene for a few moments in silence. It was the usual: barbarian warfare with a few Hun rampages mixed in for good measure. At the moment there was a pack of second graders spinning, shouting and running into one another.

"What do you think they're up to?" asked Tre. "It looks like chaos out there."

Armin nodded. "That's right."

"What's right?"

"That's the name of the game."

"What is? I just said it looked like chaos."

"Exactly," said Armin. "It's Chaos. Did you ever play that at your old school?"

"Play what? I don't get it. What they're doing looks like total nonsense to me."

Micah shook his head. "No, the second graders only play Nonsense on Tuesdays and Thursdays."

Tre sighed. "I'm so confused."

Lydia nodded at him. "We all are."

The Rules of Chaos

1. Everybody who's not playing the game is "it."

2. Everyone who *is* playing has to close their eyes and spin around twelve times. If you can keep your lunch down, you get three bonus points!

3. Run backwards as fast as you can. Whatever you do, don't look behind you!

4. If someone who's "it" tags you, you're frozen. You must lie down and scream at the top of your lungs until you're unfrozen by someone else who's "it." Since those who are "it" are not playing the game, no one's allowed to tell them that they're in charge of unfreezing people.

5. If you're frozen in the middle of a field where kids are playing a game—say, soccer or football—you get five bonus points! Every time someone yells at you to get out of the way, give yourself an extra point!

6. The winner is anyone who's still playing by the end of recess.

"It's really not that complicated—" Micah started to explain. But before he could go any farther, Hanz showed up. He pushed through Micah, Lydia, and Armin to talk to Tre, smiling his most suck-uppy, annoying smile.

Hanz looked Tre up and down. "It is clear zat you are rich like me. Let us hang out and talk about rich-people zings."

"Umm . . . ," said Tre.

"You know, like how sad it is when ze butler does not put enough of ze sprinkles on ze sundae."

"Okay . . . ," said Tre.

"Or vhat you do vhen your robot dog runs avay."

"Actually, I don't—"

"Or how to get ze rocket fuel stains out of your favorite jet-pack suit."

"Er . . . maybe I could catch you later?" said Tre.

Hanz shrugged and started to walk away. "If I vere you, I vould not spend too much time vith zese veirdos. You don't vant to get loser stink on you."

Tre looked at Micah in confusion. But before he

could ask any questions about Hanz, suddenly Chet was there.

"So, what are you?" Chet asked.

Tre shrugged. "Excuse me?"

"Are you a nerd? A jock? A geek? A bully? A rich German?"

"Hmm . . . Totally not the last one. I'm not sure about the others," Tre said. "Do I have to pick one?"

"Not right away. But don't take too long. It's better to choose than to have it chosen for you."

Then, without another word, Chet spun around and hurried away.

Lydia raised her eyebrows and nodded. "That was surprisingly wise."

Micah could tell Tre's head was spinning. But before he could ask any questions, Tre was immediately distracted by the sight of Gabe, once again, being Gabe.

"*Now* what's that dude doing?" Tre asked.

Lydia shook her head. "We never know."

"I think he's trying to get gum off the bottom of

his shoe," said Armin. "But now his shoe is somehow stuck to his ear."

Tre squinched up his eyes. "How does he bend that way?"

"We've found that it's better not to ask too many questions about Gabe," said Armin. "The mystery's half the fun!"

Tre shook his head slowly, eyes wide with wonder. "You've got a lot of gnarly kids around here."

Lydia nodded. "You have no idea."

Who IS This Kid?!

So much for steering clear of the new kid. He actually came up and introduced himself to us at recess today. Who does that?!

He seems nice enough, but there's something about him. I can't quite put my finger on it but I have lots of questions. Like, why does he carry around that skateboard? I never see him ride it!

Lydia and Armin seemed happy to hang out with him. Don't we have enough friends already? He'd better not move in on my territory.

Don't look out only for your own interests, but take an interest in others, too.
Philippians 2:4 (NLT)

▷ **What would YOU do if a new kid wanted to join your friend group?**

▷ **What do YOU think Micah should do about his bad feelings toward Tre?**

CHAPTER THREE

The next day, in the lunchroom, liver and beet hoagies were on the menu. Thankfully, Micah's mom had packed him a meal, so he didn't have to eat one. But the hoagies stunk up the cafeteria so bad they infected everything in their path anyway. Even Micah's cold pizza—usually his favorite—now had a subtle beet aftertaste.

Since he was a lunch bringer rather than a lunch buyer, Micah was one of the first fifth graders in the cafeteria. But there were a handful of other kids already sitting down. Steven Chang, the first kid in his seat, was slurping up his lime Jell-O with a straw. And at a table in the far corner of the room, Minerva Martinez was making a replica of Abe Lincoln's log cabin out of baby carrots. Micah joined Lydia at the same table they always sat at, right in the middle, where they'd soon be joined by Armin, and maybe Gabe.

A minute later, Tre walked in. He was carrying a bagged lunch and looking from table to table. By that point a few tables were starting to fill up, but there were still some that were completely empty. Micah figured Tre would probably pick one of those. It was too much pressure for a new kid to force himself on a lunch group—you never knew if you'd be sitting in a table that had all its seats already saved. Then you'd be asked to move, a mark of shame if there ever was one.

Choosing a lunch table at the beginning of the school year is one of the three toughest decisions a fifth grader ever has to face. Once you make that choice, there's no going back—you're stuck there for the rest of the year. (The other two, by the way, are what to do for your science fair project when your dad won't let you make another volcano, and what to wear for school pictures. For some reason, moms keep those things forever!)

All of a sudden, Micah got that weird feeling that he was supposed to invite the new kid to eat with him. Micah hated that feeling and wanted to do whatever it would take to make it go away. But he also hated the thought of messing with his lunch table. Lunch was one of the best parts of his day, and now this new kid was going to come in and stir things up. Lunch table chemistry was too delicate to mess with!

Before Micah could overcome his internal struggle, Armin walked up, waved his hand to get Tre's attention, and motioned him over.

"Hey."

"Hey. You can sit here if you want," Armin said, sitting down.

"Thanks, bruh."

Tre sat down. Micah and his friends ate in silence for a few seconds.

"What's that smell?" Tre asked.

"It's the school lunch," Lydia answered in disgust.

"But what *is* it?"

"Liver and beet hoagies."

"Wow. It smells like something you'd only eat if you were, like, being punished or something. Did the school do something wrong?"

"Yeah. It hired bad cooks," Micah quipped.

Tre nodded and tried to hold his own sandwich as close to his nose as he could to block the smell. Judging from the purple stains leaking through the top of the bread, Micah guessed it was peanut butter and jelly. An absolute classic.

"So, what do you like to do for fun?" Tre asked.

Micah shrugged. "Video games mostly. I'm at the fourteenth level of *Captain Karate Dino Cop 4* . . . That's the one where—"

"Where Captain Eradicus gets his time-slurping powers and you surf the fourth dimension!" Tre broke in. "That's totally rad! I'm only on level 11."

"Oh." Micah nodded. "That's cool. You'll get there before long."

"We don't *all* play video games," Lydia clarified. She still hadn't looked up from her hoagie. She lifted the bun carefully with her fork and examined the ingredients like a chemist in a crime lab. Micah couldn't blame her. A crime against good taste had clearly been committed that day.

"I saw there's a sign-up sheet for the spring play," said Tre. "You guys thinking about signing up?"

"Probably not," said Micah quickly. He hoped the subject would change.

Armin shrugged. "I'm thinking about it. We were all in Miss Petunia's play in the fall."

"Oh yeah?" Tre asked. "What was it called?"

"*Don't You Carrot All?*" Armin answered.

"Um, yeah . . . I do care." Tre looked confused. "That's why I asked."

"No, I wasn't saying you don't care. That was the name of the play. *Don't You Carrot All?* Get it? It's a play on words. Miss Petunia likes that sort of thing."

"Oh, okay. I don't think I've seen that one," Tre responded.

"You wouldn't have," Lydia answered, still without looking up. She was now carefully sniffing each square inch of her hoagie, perhaps trying to detect traces of poison.

"What were your roles in the play?" Tre asked, looking directly at Micah first.

"I was an . . ." He hesitated. It wasn't an easy thing to admit. ". . . artichoke."

"I was a box of raisins!" Armin said proudly. "And Lydia was cream of mushroom soup."

Tre nodded thoughtfully. "That sounds awesome. I'd love to read the script sometime. Who wrote the play?"

"Miss Petunia," said Lydia, now taking a nibble

off the corner of her bun. "She writes all our plays. They're food based."

"Food based?" Tre asked. "Never heard of a food-based play before."

Micah shrugged. "It's pretty self-explanatory. I bet it's exactly what you're picturing."

"That's cool," said Tre. "Acting's totally rad."

Suddenly Micah felt a little embarrassed he'd been sitting with Tre all this time and hadn't asked him what he liked to do. He wasn't keen on making Tre feel *too* welcome, but he also didn't want to be rude. Quite the balancing act.

At the very least he felt like the moment required a follow-up question. "So, what kind of acting have you done before?"

Tre wiped some jelly off his lip with a napkin. "Just like you dudes, I've totally rocked some school plays. But I haven't had the chance to do any, like, food-based ones."

It was strange. A sentence like that from anyone else would have been dripping with sarcasm. But it really sounded to Micah like Tre was sincerely interested in the opportunity. Who was this weirdo, anyway?

But Tre was still talking, leaving Micah no time to analyze him in his head.

" . . . and I acted in a commercial once that was on TV."

"Wait!" said Lydia.

"What did you just say?" asked Armin.

"Did I hear what I thought I heard?" said Katie, who'd been sitting at the next table, but was now right at Tre's side.

"Did someone say they were on television?" asked Makayla, from two tables over.

Suddenly the whole lunchroom was buzzing. Girls and boys shouted across the room at one another to verify what they thought they'd heard, and dozens of them hopped out of their seats to come closer to Tre's table. Somehow a cameraman even showed up out of nowhere, along with PB and J, New Leaf Elementary's student celebrity correspondents. Micah wondered how it was even possible they could get a scoop that quickly!

Tre didn't seem to notice. He just looked at Micah and kept talking. "Speaking of which, I wanted to ask you something . . ."

But there was no way for him to get another word out. PB and J were now right by his side, shoving Micah out of the way as they lifted Tre up out of his seat.

Breaking news from fifth-grade lunch!" said PB into a microphone.

"That's right!" said J. "We've got a brand-new student celebrity on our hands!"

"Tre Buzznik is his name, and he's been in plays, commercials, and even a TV show!"

"Did you say a TV show, PB?"

"You heard me right, J!"

"Tre, how does it feel to be the hottest thing at New Leaf since Meghan Lumpke moved away?"

"And she was amazing!" said J. "She could face paint a flower on her own cheek without even looking in the mirror!"

"What a star!"

"But you!" said J. "Commercials? Television shows? Care to comment?"

"Well . . . ," said Tre, blushing, "actually, I was, like, totally in the middle of talking to—"

"We realize how valuable your time must be," said J. "But your fans have a right to know!"

"You're hot! You're a celebrity!" said PB. "You belong to us now!"

"Isn't that marvelous?" asked J.

"I guess, but—"

"Tell us all about the TV shows and movies you've been in!" said PB.

"And all the famous celebrities you know!" said J.

"Well . . ." Tre paused. "A lot of the stuff I'm in has been indie projects. They're hard to find. Besides, I really hate to brag about stuff like that. That's just not how I roll, ya know."

Micah stared at Tre skeptically. Really? What fifth grader wouldn't want to brag about being a movie star? That didn't seem normal at all.

But J wouldn't give up. "Just give us one movie title! Or a single TV show!"

Things That Are Faster Than a Fifth-Grade Rumor

- The speed of pizza slices disappearing at an elementary school pizza party
- The speed of Audrey coming up with a sarcastic remark as soon as Micah says something dumb
- The speed of light
- The speed of sound
- The speed of smell (Smell is surprisingly fast. Within twelve seconds of a lunch lady removing the plastic wrap from a liver and beet hoagie, the smell will pass through the entire building—including Mr. Beaker's science lab, somehow covering up the odor of chemical explosions and dissected worms.)

And that's about it. There's not much faster than a rumor in fifth grade.

Suddenly, the room exploded with sound—a heart-stoppingly loud clanging noise that hurt their ears and was nearly impossible to talk over. Almost immediately, the clanging was accompanied by the screaming, shouting, and in some cases cheering of eighty-seven fifth graders.

It took Micah a moment to figure out what was happening. Was somebody starting a revolution? Was the school under alien attack? Had one of Mr. Beaker's experiments finally busted through the space-time continuum? What could it possibly be?

"Fire alarm!" Mr. Turtell shouted.

Oh yeah. That made sense.

"Everybody calm down!" Mr. Turtell waved his arms in the air to get people's attention. "Head to the properly marked exits!"

The excitement of getting to go outside before their regularly scheduled recess passed like a wave of giddiness through the fifth graders. Micah watched everyone completely ignore Mr. Turtell's first instruction (nobody was even *trying* to calm down) and mostly ignore his second instruction (one of the exits the students funneled through was missing the letter *T*. Properly marked indeed!)

As Micah flooded through the exit, he looked around for his friends. They were nowhere to be seen. In an out-of-control crowd like this one, you rarely get to choose your travel companions. You are a piece of driftwood on a fast-flowing river, and either you go along with the flow, or you get pummeled by the current.

Along with the blaring alarm, the constant drone of Mr. Turtell's voice carried through the crowd. "Single file. Keep it orderly. Inside voices."

Three more instructions for the fifth graders to ignore. But it didn't seem to bother Mr. Turtell. Micah wondered if he was on autopilot, saying the things teachers were supposed to say in such situations, assuming they would be ignored.

But there was no time to ponder—the current had Micah in its grip. Out of the lunchroom and into the hallway Micah flowed, classmates on his left and right, and in front and behind. He flowed past encouraging wall posters telling him to "Seize the day" and "Eat more green foods." (He wondered briefly if this was the reason for Steven Chang's obsession with lime Jell-O.)

He flowed past the teacher's lounge, its door wide-open (which was almost never the case), catching a glimpse inside the mysterious room. It was much less exciting than he'd imagined. Why no flat-screen TV? Why no soft-serve ice cream machine? Did they even understand the point of having their own lounge?

He flowed past the principal's office and caught a glimpse of Mr. Drury still sitting at his desk, typing away at his computer. Either this was just a routine drill, or Mr. Drury was a VERY dedicated principal.

But no time to worry about that, because just a few seconds later he flowed through the main doors of the school and out into the beautiful world outside.

The wide-open world! The real world! The free world!

A world of blue skies and tall trees and chirping birds and . . .

Mounds of snow on the ground?

Oh yeah. It was winter. And Micah had left his coat in the lunchroom.

Rats.

All around him kids were running around, going crazy. Boys and girls were skipping and laughing and jumping up and down in each other's arms. They were only getting an extra five minutes of recess, since their lunch was almost over by the time the alarm went off, but you would have thought they were prisoners who'd been granted five years off their life sentences. (But certainly *not* for good behavior.)

"Five extra minutes!" Katie shouted.

"I can't believe this is really happening!" Makayla screamed.

"This is the greatest day of my life!" Eric yelled.

Micah looked around for Armin and Lydia but didn't see them right away. He did catch a glimpse of Gabe on the ground. "Why isn't anybody else rolling?" Gabe shouted. "Stop, drop, and roll, people, roll! Didn't fireman Pete teach you anything?"

Beyond Gabe there was a large huddle of fifth graders all pressed together. He could see Armin and Lydia on the edge of the crowd, staring toward the middle. As Micah came near, he realized it was a press conference. Tre was in the center, with PB and J still asking questions. Apparently even a fire alarm couldn't slow down the intrepid celebrity correspondents.

"How about we get some footage of you riding your board, Tre?" PB asked him.

"Can't today, bruh. Not wearing the right laces."

Micah walked up to Armin and Lydia. "Are you kidding me?" he asked.

They both peeled away from the crowd and walked toward the playground. Lydia shrugged. "If someone's going to get this kind of attention, at least it's a nice guy like Tre."

"I wonder," said Micah. Something about the way Tre answered PB's skateboarding request once again felt suspicious to him. Who wouldn't want to show off in front of the camera?

"About?" Armin asked.

Micah had no idea how to answer that question. He hadn't really thought it through and didn't want to accuse Tre of anything just yet. "Stuff," he said weakly.

"Don't wonder too much," Lydia said. "We've got a movie to plan."

As they headed over to their favorite spot under the tree, Micah shivering in his long-sleeve T-shirt, he caught a glimpse of Chet kicking a little kid off a swing.

"Fire drills are awesome!" Chet said to no one in particular. "And I didn't even have to pull the alarm myself this time!"

This Is NOT a Drill

Well . . . it's happening. This kid is taking over New Leaf Elementary. Not only is he "dreamy" (still not sure what that means), cool, and talented—he's actually been on real live TV! Could things possibly get any worse?

I've got to do something to turn things around, and fast! Before you know it, my friends won't even remember my name.

Micah who?

Don't worry about anything; pray about everything. Tell God what you need, and thank him for all he has done.
Philippians 4:6 (NLT)

▷ **Why do YOU think Micah is feeling so anxious about Tre?**

▷ **What do YOU think Micah should do before his emotions spin out of control?**

CHAPTER FOUR

Another day, another recess. Today, there were the usual games of soccer, basketball, Chaos, and, of course, a handful of cootie-infested girls chasing a contingent of boys who had yet to get their cootie shots. Meanwhile, Chet was playing dodgeball with half a dozen nerds who didn't want to. They ran away and tried to hide as he threw balls at them as hard as he could. (Unlike most games, one can be forced into playing dodgeball against one's will.)

Others shouted and laughed as they threw snowballs at one another, claiming it was albino dinosaur poop. And maybe it was. Who was Micah to argue?

But after a tough morning of learning, all Micah wanted to do was play a friendly game of four square with his buddies. There was something particularly soothing about four square. The rhythmic back-and-forth pattern of the four players and the bouncing ball was like some kind of complex and beautiful dance. The only difference, to Micah, was that dances were dumb and four square was awesome.

The other thing Micah liked about four square was the fact that it needed four people and he had three friends: Armin, Lydia, and Gabe, so the math worked.

The server got to name the rules, and as Lydia grabbed the ball for her turn to serve, she called, "No slamma jamma, but light and fluffy is on the table." That was four square for, "Let's keep it gentle." Which was okay with Micah. When things got rough, he usually lost to Armin.

They'd been playing for five minutes and gotten eighty-seven hits in a row—only five shy of their record—when Gabe lost track and let the ball slip by him.

"What happened there?" Micah asked.

"What happened to what?" Gabe asked back. He clearly wasn't paying attention. In fact, he wasn't looking at Micah or the ball. His gaze was going back and forth, and then he wandered off slowly in a winding path.

"What's he doing?" Micah asked.

"I think he's following that butterfly," said Armin.

Micah followed Armin's pointing finger and saw something shiny drifting in the air a few feet off the ground.

"That's not a butterfly," said Lydia. "It's just a silver gum wrapper blowing in the breeze."

Armin nodded. "Either way, Gabe's gone now. It's impossible to get him back once he's seen something shiny."

"So, does that mean we're done playing?" Lydia asked.

"Let's look around to see if anybody's wandering the playground, looking for something to do," said Micah.

But Micah regretted his words almost immediately. Tre was heading their way, and Micah suspected he'd probably be up for a game of four square.

"Hey Tre," said Lydia and Armin, almost at the same time.

"Hey guys. Micah, I was totally looking for you."

"Oh yeah? Why's that?"

"I was bummed how PB and J cornered me yesterday in the middle of our conversation. I tried to get away several times, but they can be hard to shake, if you know what I mean."

"You don't say," said Lydia. Unlike Tre, sarcasm was her second language.

"Mind if I join you?" Tre stepped into position on the four square court before they could answer. "I love four square." Their game continued, but for some reason, Micah wasn't all that into it anymore.

"Anyway, I had a question I wanted to ask you," Tre went on while passing the ball. "The other day, you guys mentioned you were making a movie. Micah, I think they said you're the director. So . . ."

He almost looked nervous.

"So . . . ," Lydia encouraged him. Micah could guess what she wanted him to ask.

"So . . . ," Tre started again, "I was wondering if you happen to need any more actors."

It was Micah's turn to catch the ball. He stood in his square in stunned silence, and it dropped to the ground.

"Of course we do!" said Lydia and Armin, again practically at the same time.

"We could *definitely* use the help," Lydia added.

Micah found himself feeling offended, but he wasn't quite sure why. Lydia wasn't wrong. They could definitely use more actors. When it came to filling the necessary roles of a fantasy epic, it turned out having only four actors and a dog wasn't quite enough. They were all stretched a little thin.

But the movie was Micah's thing—he was in charge. And now this new kid might come in and shake things up. He liked being in charge and didn't want anybody stealing his thunder. And unfortunately, he could already see Tre had Lydia's full attention.

Tre looked at Micah, who hadn't said anything yet. It was hard not to notice.

"Sure," he finally answered.

Tre smiled. "Rad!"

Lydia beamed. "We're filming tonight after school at Pondbridge Park."

"Maybe you can take one of my parts," said Armin. "There was a scene where I was going to have to sword fight with myself. But I think that was going to be hard to pull off."

Lydia nodded. "Especially when you have to chop off your own head."

"Fine." Micah shrugged. "But I could have totally made it work in editing."

Micah thought school would never end that day. The clock toyed with him for hours, but eventually it got around to 3:30. He rushed out the door having almost forgotten his coat once again, but slowed down just long enough to grab it, run home to get his dog, and then head to Pondbridge Park.

And now here he was, standing on a small hill with trees all around him, envisioning the moviemaking magic that was about to happen. The sky was bright blue, and a strong breeze was blowing around leaves and script pages and fake mustaches.

It was cold outside, as one would expect on a windy January day, but Micah could hardly feel it. He was just so excited to finally get to start filming! He loved movies so much, and to make one with his best friends was a dream come true.

The only thing that had the potential to bring him down—just the teensiest bit—was the presence of his sister, Audrey. Audrey was not the type of girl who willingly participated in any of her brother's projects. Her father was making her help because of one too many instances of eye-rolling at the dinner table. Being in Micah's movie was pure punishment for her, and it showed all over her face. Ironically, with an eye roll.

And Micah, taking advantage of the situation, had given her the part of the swamp monster. She was covered in boils (oatmeal) and wore a long, green wig. Other than that, she wore her own clothes, which, remarkably, looked to Micah like something a swamp monster would wear anyway.

Micah wasn't about to let his sister's bad attitude distract him. He had a schedule to keep!

"Let's get started," Micah announced to Armin, Lydia, Gabe, and his less-than-enthusiastic sibling. "Did everybody get the shooting schedules I sent out?"

"Yeah, but I don't understand why we're doing the scenes out of order," said Armin. "Why don't we just shoot them in the regular order? You know: scene 1 then scene 2 then scene 3, etc.?"

"First of all," Micah said, "we've got to film all the scenes with my sister right away. My dad's only making Audrey be in the movie for a couple days. Then her punishment ends and she's free to go."

"Bummer," said Gabe sincerely.

"Bummer," said Audrey sarcastically.

Micah ignored them. "Second of all, the best movies are always shot out of order. It's just the way it's done in Hollywood."

"Why?" Armin asked.

"No idea," said Micah. "Anyway, let's get going. We're starting with scene 3 when the swamp monster gets attacked. Armin, can you slip that mane and saddle on your trusty steed?"

"On my what?"

"Your trusty steed. Barnabas. He's going to be Helo's horse for this scene. His mane and saddle are right there by camera 2."

"But Helo will look ridiculous! Barnabas is barely taller than my knees. You told me Helo would look awesome!"

Audrey nodded. "Plus, if Helo tries to sit on his trusty steed's back, he'll snap him like a twig. Then my mom will kill Helo."

"Nobody's sitting on Barnabas!" Micah shouted. "You'll just stand beside him, Armin. Trust me. It'll look great. I learned how to do these types of special effects with camera angles. And I'll fix anything that doesn't look right in editing."

Armin got Barnabas fully dressed while Micah adjusted one of the cameras. By the time Micah turned around, there was a perfect little pony standing right beside him.

Well, maybe not perfect, but he looked pretty good. Micah studied his dog pony as he stepped back.

If you squinted your eyes just right.

And stepped far enough back.

And tried not to look directly at him.

Micah shook it off. Anything could be fixed in editing.

"Okay. Cameras rolling," said Micah. "Now, Armin, you're walking your horse through the woods, desperately searching for Eleandor, the elf princess. You know she's in trouble but have no idea where she is—Brilliant, Armin! That's good searching! I like how you're holding your hand to your forehead like that, looking back and forth!"

Micah was watching Armin and Barnabas on the screen, and they actually looked pretty good. "Okay, cameras still rolling. Now, Audrey, this is the swamp monster's first appearance. You jump out from behind that tree, hold your hand out, and scream, 'STOP!'"

Audrey sauntered out from behind the tree and said, "Stop."

It was not screamed.

It was not shouted.

It was not even interjected.

It was spoken with all the passion of a child telling his mom that, no, he supposed he didn't really *need* another scoop of ice cream.

"Cut!" Micah shouted. "Audrey, let's try that again, but this time with more enthusiasm."

"Whatever."

She rolled her eyes.

Micah ignored her.

"Okay," said Micah. "Take two. Cameras rolling."

Audrey stepped quickly out from behind the tree and said, "Stop!"

Still not screamed or shouted. But this time it did seem a little more like an interjection. It was the tone your mom takes with you just *before* she starts shouting. Like when she says, "Stop. You are *not* eating another bowl of ice cream. It's bedtime."

And in Micah's mind, this was probably as good as he was going to get from his sister.

"Okay, fine. Now I'm going to move my camera over here so I can get a better angle of you two fighting. Audrey, you hurl those green globs of cheese at Armin, and Armin you try to deflect them with your sword."

This, it turned out, Audrey was very willing to do. Soon Armin was covered in green goop. It's not easy to deflect cheese with a sword.

"Stop hitting my helmet!" said Armin. "You keep knocking it over my eyes, and then I can't see!"

"Okay," said Micah. "Cut. I think I got enough good angles. It looks awesome on screen! Now, Armin, you run away, injured but undeterred from your quest. Until, finally, you see Eleandor in the big

oak tree. At first you think she's all alone, and you smile. (Brilliant! You're really good at this, Armin!) But then you see the hunchback also in the tree, holding her hostage."

Micah looked at Lydia on his screen. Though not in costume today (her mom was making it from scratch), he could already envision her in her long, green dress. She really would look like an elf princess, perched on her branch twenty feet above the ground. Then he looked at Gabe. Something was off.

"Gabe, push your backpack around so it's under the back of your cape, not the front. Right now you look more like Santa Claus than a hunchback."

Gabe spun it around. Not bad.

"Are you sure you don't want Url the hunchback to moan like a whale?" he asked. "That could be, like, his thing."

"I'm sure," said Micah.

"Okay. Tell me when to go."

"Cameras rolling, and . . . go."

"You'll never claw your way back onto the

throne of Andoria!" Gabe said. "You think you're better than me, but you're not! The kingdom should have been mine from the start—you never deserved it!"

Gabe spoke in a horrifyingly creepy, guttural drawl. It was terrible and awesome all at the same time. He'd really listened to Micah's notes from their last rehearsal. Perfect!

"That's what you think," said Lydia proudly. "But Helo will come for me. I know it! You'll never get away with such treachery!"

"Cut! Perfect!" shouted Micah. "I need to move the camera again for your fight in the treetop. Gabe, where on earth did you come up with that amazing accent?"

Gabe shrugged. "It's how my great-grandmother Pearl Blocnicek talks. She's from east Bulgaria by way of Tennessee. She's hilarious. And terrifying. One time I spent the night at her house, and she didn't have anything to fix for breakfast except noodle boxes, so she made me eat half a box."

"That doesn't sound like such a big deal," said Armin. "I wouldn't mind eating noodles for breakfast."

"No, there weren't any noodles left. She made me eat half the *box*."

"Oh." Micah didn't know what else to say to this.

He moved camera 2 so it was right below the tree, looking up into it at Lydia and Gabe. "Okay. Now you two fight in the tree."

A very strange thing to ask two people to do, Micah realized. But such was the life of a director.

He watched the screen to see what the cameras were catching. Not bad! Not bad at all. *Maybe I'm actually good at this*, Micah thought. *If I can get into the Middletown Film Festival . . .*

Micah watched Eleandor and Url fake punch each other several times, and then Url grabbed Eleandor by the arm while Eleandor grabbed Url by the hair. Their fight was slower and more careful than usual for an elf princess and a hunchback, but Micah wasn't surprised. They were trying to keep their balance up in a tree so they didn't fall at the wrong moment. And besides, Micah could speed it up in editing.

But then, as Micah watched the battle, the big moment came! Url yanked his hair free of Eleandor's grasp. (She ended up with a small patch of hunchback hair in her fist. Nice!) Then he twisted her arm until she had to spin herself around. But there was no more room on the branch to spin on!

Micah watched Eleandor stand there on one foot for a split second, and then saw her leg give way. Down she fell! All three cameras caught her in midair, screaming as she tumbled to the ground twenty feet below!

It was amazing!

It was incredible!

It was perfect in every way!

Perfect, that is, except for the boy who came out of nowhere, screaming and running into the shot.

"Cut!" Micah shouted. "Rats! Now we have to film that scene all over again."

You Call That Help?!

Urghhhhh!

First Tre weasels his way into my movie, and then he manages to ruin a perfectly executed scene. Seriously?!

Why does this kid insist on messing up my life? Now we have to film the scene all over again. So much for Tre "helping" with my movie. He's made it more work!

Get rid of all bitterness . . . Instead, be kind to each other, tenderhearted, forgiving one another, just as God through Christ has forgiven you.
Ephesians 4:31-32 (NLT)

▷ **How do YOU think Micah should respond to Tre's unfortunate entrance?**

▷ **Do YOU think Micah needs to change his perspective on Tre? Why?**

CHAPTER FIVE

Micah stared at the kid who had barged onto the scene, ruining his shot. It was Tre, of course. He should have suspected.

Tre wore a medieval helmet, a shield, a weathered cloak, and leather boots that looked like they'd seen a few village raids in their day. Micah couldn't help but admit to himself that he looked terrific—you couldn't even see jeans or a sweatshirt under the cloak. There would hardly be anything for Micah to fix in editing!

Tre didn't seem to have heard Micah. He ran up to Lydia, who was just standing up from what looked like a pile of leaves underneath the oak tree. "Are you all right? Did you, like, break a bone or anything?"

"I'm fine." Lydia brushed a layer of leaves off the place where she'd landed. "See. There's a trampoline under there. We had it all figured out."

"Nice!" Tre looked over at Micah. "You guys are pretty good at this stuff."

"You're late," Micah said.

"So sorry, bruh. This costume took a little longer to put together than I thought it would." Tre really did seem to feel bad about being late.

"It's okay," Lydia assured him, like she had any right to speak for the director. "That costume is amazing! You . . . er, I mean . . . your costume is well worth the wait." Lydia blushed.

Micah rolled his eyes. He didn't want to admit it, but Tre's costume was pretty great.

"Can I see that shot on screen?" Tre asked.

Micah rewound the video and let him have a look, narrating as they watched. "See? There are some great shots of the elf princess and the hunchback, wrestling high above the ground. And then right there is where the hunchback gets the advantage and the princess starts to fall. There's a perfect shot of her screaming all the way to the ground. And then that's where you came into the scene, screaming and ruining everything."

"Oh. Sorry, bruh. But it's, like, a totally amazing scene! Maybe I could even send a few rough cuts to some dudes I know in the business. When you're all done, I'd be stoked to try to help you get it in the film festival!"

"That would be amazing," said Armin. "We've been talking about trying to do that, but we don't have any connections."

"Do you really think it's good?" Micah asked. "I can't tell if you're being sarcastic or not." Micah was encouraged but a little suspicious. *Who could Tre possibly know in the Middletown movie business?*

"Of course I think it's good! It's awesome! And why does everybody keep thinking I'm being sarcastic all the time?"

Lydia shrugged. "Sarcasm is pretty popular around here."

"Because it's awesome," Audrey said. Not a bit sarcastically.

"You look great, Tre," said Armin.

Gabe lifted Tre's helmet off and looked closely at his head. "Yeah, terrific costume. This wig is amazing!"

"It's my real hair."

"Even better! Just don't let Lydia yank on it too hard."

"Thanks for the warning."

"Do you like my costume?" Gabe asked. "I'm a hunchback!"

"Totally, bruh! It's one of the best hunchback costumes I've ever seen," Tre answered. "You really look deformed!"

"Thanks!" Gabe reached around to his back and felt around under his cape. "Anybody want a Twizzler? I've been keeping snacks in my hunch. I've got fruit gummies, nutty bars, even some homemade granola!"

Audrey made a face. "That's disgusting."

But everyone else took a short Twizzler break.

"We're really glad to have you here, Tre," Lydia said after they reshot the scene of her falling out of the tree. "Micah, wouldn't Tre be great in the duel in scene 5? Like Armin mentioned earlier, right now he has to sword fight against himself."

"I guess we could think about it," said Micah. "But it's a little late for changes."

"Come on, Micah!" said Armin. "You know we need him. Remember the last time I tried to sword fight with myself? I pulled my shoulder out of socket."

"But we don't even know if Tre knows how to sword fight," said Micah.

"Do you?" Lydia asked.

"I'm only trained in Eastern Deluvian freestyle fencing. Are you dudes comfortable with that dueling style?"

Micah had no idea what Tre was talking about. "Um . . . well . . . okay. I guess we could give it a try and see if it works with the style we were already using."

"Great!" Armin said to Tre. "Maybe you can show me some good moves. The hunchback and I have to sword fight in the next scene."

As Tre worked with Armin and Gabe on sword-fighting techniques, Micah and Lydia set up the cameras and also made a small fort out of sticks for the swamp monster's home. Audrey mostly just petted Barnabas and looked at her phone.

All the while, Micah could hear Tre saying complicated-sounding sword-fighting terms. ("That's where you should totally try the highlander twist, Armin. And then, Gabe, you counter that move with an old classic: the Spanish fist bump. Great job, dude! Okay, Armin, now twist into the allemande left.")

"Isn't allemande left a square-dancing move?" Micah asked no one in particular. No one in particular paid any attention to him.

Finally, Micah and Lydia had the cameras set up and Armin and Gabe were ready to go. "Okay, act 2, scene 4," said Micah. "Cameras rolling."

Url the hunchback jumped out from behind a blackberry bush—startling two squirrels up a tree in the process—and attacked Helo. Helo was caught unprepared, and Url had the upper hand for a moment. But Helo was no untrained farmhand— he was a proud and lonesome warrior who knew his way around a sword fight!

Micah had to admit, he really *did* look like he knew his way around a sword fight. And so did the hunchback, for that matter. They looked ten times better than when they'd practiced this fight just the day before. Maybe Tre really knew a thing or two.

Round and round they dueled, parrying and thrusting and allemanding and Spanish-fist-bumping. All the moves they'd learned looked great. Micah watched it on the camera's screen, shocked how much good footage he was getting! Helo twisted Url's sword out of his hand, and then Url dove down onto the ground to retrieve it.

Everything was coming together, and the scene was almost complete. All in one shot! Micah couldn't believe how well it was going.

But as Url lay on the ground, his hand fumbling through the leaves for his sword, an unexpected movement caught Micah's eye.

At the top of the camera's screen, one—no two—small fuzzy creatures leaped down out of nowhere toward Url.

"Aghhhhh!" Gabe yelled. "Get them off me!"

"The squirrels want the snacks!" Armin shouted.

Gabe thrashed around on the ground. "My hunch! My hunch!"

Micah ran from his camera to help Gabe, now rolling around on his belly. Two squirrels clung to Gabe's back, trying to dig under his cape for nutty bars and granola.

Suddenly Barnabas, whom Audrey was supposed to be holding, saw the squirrels and charged! Just as the dog was in mid-leap, about to land on top of the squirrels on top of the hunchback, the squirrels shot off Url and jumped onto the trunk of a tree.

Barnabas no longer had squirrels to land on, but there was still a hunchback beneath him. He caught one whiff of the goodies in Gabe's hunch and grabbed a mouthful of cape and backpack, chewing through both to get to the snacks inside.

"Cut!" Micah yelled. "Okay, people. That's a wrap! We'll get back to work tomorrow."

Micah sat with his mom, dad, and Audrey at the dinner table. They were surrounded by small boxes of delicious foods from Tom and Barbara's Asian Cuisine, one of Micah's very favorite restaurants.

Micah should have been thrilled. Despite some hiccups along the way, the first day of filming had gone well. And he had one of his favorite meals laid out before him. But still, he felt annoyed. And even worse, he was annoyed that he was annoyed, because he really had nothing to be annoyed about. How annoying.

It's just that his life had been going so well. He was making a movie with his best friends, and he was in a great routine at school and recess and lunch, and everything was finally, for once in his life, easy and comfortable. Bringing a new kid into the mix just messed everything up. Especially when everyone looked up to him and admired him. How was he supposed to be in charge of making this movie when now there was somebody else his actors were starting to listen to?

Micah grabbed a crab Rangoon. Most of the meal had been silent so far, and that made him nervous. His dad wasn't much for silence, and Micah wasn't usually too excited about the way he liked to fill it.

AUTHENTIC BOB'S
CHINESE FOOD
ENJOY THANK YOU

**My Dad's Favorite
Dinner Conversation Starters**

- "Back in my day . . ." (Usually followed by how cheap things used to be.)

- "How about that economy?" (I have no idea what this even means.)

- "Looks like weather is coming in." (Isn't weather always coming in, good or bad?)

- "Who needs a haircut?" (Please don't be me!)

- "Whatever happened to that guy in that show we used to like?" (Umm . . . ?)

- "Guess what I had for lunch from this stain on my tie!" (My personal favorite.)

Micah figured he might as well talk about what he was thinking. "So, we had a great afternoon filming my movie at the park."

"That's great, honey!" said Micah's mom.

Micah shrugged. "I guess."

"You don't seem too excited for a director who just finished a good shoot," said his dad.

"He's just miffed because there's a cool new kid at his school, and he's afraid Tre is going to steal his thunder," Audrey teased.

"That's not it." Micah was annoyed. "I'm just not sure about him. Something seems off to me."

"Are you kidding?" Audrey said. "He's the one that's off? Have you seen you and your friends lately? He's the only cool kid I've ever met in your whole grade! He could actually make your movie watchable."

Uh-oh. Micah didn't know what to do with this. Now even Audrey was on "Team Tre." She thought he was cool, and she never liked any of his friends. She was wrong about them, of course, because Micah's friends were awesome. And so, if he couldn't trust her judgment about his friends, then that meant that Tre must actually *not* be cool. Then again, Micah liked to hang out with the kids at school who weren't too "cool," so maybe, then, he should like hanging out with Tre.

Wow. His head was spinning from the logic. What was he trying to figure out again?

"You should always make room for new friends," said his mom.

His dad nodded. "Yeah, and if he can help you with your movie, all the better."

"And your movie can use all the help it can get," said Audrey.

Micah's annoyance was growing. Audrey wasn't wrong, and that made it all the worse. It was all just . . . just . . .

All of a sudden, he blurted out, "Cut! That's a wrap!"

Everybody stared at him.

"Umm . . . Micah?" his dad said. "That's not how dinner works."

Team Tre

Sometimes I wish my life took place on a movie set so I could shout, "CUT" every time I wanted to take a break. But no, we're living real life here, and there's no breaks for these actors . . . er, I mean, kids.

It seems everyone—including my parents and my sister—are on Team Tre right now. What is it about that kid?!

I still think he's a little too good to be true. No one is that perfect. There's got to be more going on than meets the eye. I wish everyone would stop obsessing so much about his stellar qualities and see him from my perspective.

For wherever there is jealousy and selfish ambition, there you will find disorder . . .
James 3:16 (NLT)

▷ **Have YOU ever wanted to take a break from life's drama? What did you do?**

▷ **What do YOU think Micah should do when he's overwhelmed with anxiety?**

CHAPTER SIX

It was Saturday. The best day of the week for budding young directors who also happen to still be in elementary school. It had been a busy morning, packed with exciting sword fights, poisoned gruel, an evil step-elf, and Barnabas dressed as a moat dragon.

All morning Tre had been an expert in everything: how to light the inside of a swamp monster's hut, the secret to making poison cauldrons glow, and the best way to make it look like you're riding a dog . . . er . . . pony, even if you're really just running alongside it. Micah had to admit that Tre was raising the whole production up a notch. He even gave him a few lines in one of the fight scenes, and he did this amazing fake British accent that made Micah's script sound like Shakespeare!

Micah couldn't help but wonder where Tre had picked up all these Hollywood secrets. Maybe Tre had more experience than he let on.

After four hours of filming, they had to be done for the day. Tre's mom made him come home for lunch, and Gabe had to go to the vet to have his possum neutered (Micah wasn't sure what this meant, but didn't want to ask). So, it was just Micah, Armin, and Lydia who headed downtown to their favorite food truck: Fry It Up and Put It on a Stick.

The food truck was parked in the vacant lot right behind the Gas & Save, which was the truck's winter home. In warm weather it traveled to all the tristate area's biggest festivals—Medieval Fest, Monster Truck Fest, Weiner Dog Fest, Stinky Cheese Fest, etc.—so Middletown residents only got to enjoy its services for a few months of the year. As one would expect on a Saturday at lunchtime, there were already several dozen people in line.

You might think at a place like Fry It Up, you'd only be able to order stuff like corn dogs and cheese curds and maybe the occasional potato wedge. But no! This was a real think-outside-the-box establishment. They'd fry up *anything* and put it on a stick!

A Few Surprising Menu Items at Fry It Up and Put It on a Stick

- Pickles

- Twizzlers

- Hard-Boiled Eggs

- Peanut M&M's

- Rice Krispies Treats

- Bubblicious Bubblegum

- Bring Your Own Meat from Home. We'll provide the stick!

- Fried Chicken (This might not sound surprising at first. You're probably thinking to yourself, "Of course they'd serve fried chicken on a stick." But you're not thinking big enough. It's not just fried chicken on a stick. It's fried fried chicken on a stick. In other words, you take a piece of fried chicken, and then you fry it and put it on a stick. Brilliant!)

After a terrific morning of filming, an empty Saturday afternoon stretched out before him, and a chance to eat a Fry It Up delicacy, Micah should have been on top of the world.

And he was.

Almost.

Except there was just one little thing that was still haunting the back of his mind.

Micah swallowed a bite of his fried peanut-butter-and-jelly-on-a-stick. "Seriously, guys. Do you really think there's nothing fishy about Tre?"

"What are you talking about, Micah?" asked Armin, wiping fried pickle off his chin. "Tre's great! He's so talented, but not at all cocky or annoying."

"Seriously, Micah," said Lydia. "I don't know why you have such a problem with him."

"Did you see him helping Gabe figure out a lyre solo during the royal banquet scene today?" Armin asked. "Who plays the lyre? We just brought it to the set for decoration!"

"Yeah," said Lydia. "He's . . . perfect!"

Lydia was smitten.

Micah just shook his head. "Isn't it funny that he carries a skateboard around, but we've never seen him use it? And if he's so cool, why does he want to hang out with *us*?"

"Does it matter?! Is it *so* inconvenient to have someone around that's smart and handsome and smells good?" Lydia wondered.

Armin and Micah stared at her.

"Anyway . . . ," said Armin. "I just think you need to cut him some slack. He's a great addition to our school, and he's been so helpful with the movie."

"Now I get it!" Lydia stared wide-eyed at Micah. "You're jealous of him! Huh. Interesting. I've never seen you jealous before. Of all the bad emotions, I wonder if we're seeing you get jealous for the very first time. Let's see . . . I've seen you annoyed. And angry."

"And scared, of course," Armin added. "And we've definitely seen you confused."

"And whiny," Lydia joined back in. "And sad. And disappointed."

"And worried. And impatient. And bored."

"Don't forget lazy!"

"Hey!" Micah said. "You can stop this list anytime now."

"Oh. Sorry," said Lydia. "Where were we? Yeah, that's it: you're jealous."

"That's ridiculous," said Micah. "I'm not jealous. I'm just suspicious." But his brain said Armin and

Lydia might actually be making a little bit of sense. (Well, Armin at least. Lydia seemed a little *too* fond of Tre.) Still, something deep in Micah's stomach continued to tell him there was more to the story with this kid. But what was he supposed to do?

And then Micah saw it! There was a huge billboard across the street with a photo of a smart-looking woman and the words "Angel McManus, Private Investigator: When you want to learn the truth!"

"That's it!"

"What's it?"

"We'll hire a private investigator!"

"*We'll* do no such thing!" said Lydia.

Armin nodded, agreeing with Lydia.

"Okay then. *I'll* hire a private investigator," said Micah.

Lydia shook her head. "You know that's one of your dumbest ideas yet, Micah. Just think about it: if Tre doesn't have anything shady in his past, then you've wasted your money. And if he *does* have something shady, then who knows what kind of trouble he'll be in? He might not even be able to work on the movie with us anymore! And now he's absolutely necessary to the film!"

"I wouldn't say *necessary*," said Micah.

Armin and Lydia just stared at him.

Micah ignored their looks. "Whatever. I just have to know his story!"

"I'm with Lydia," said Armin. "It's just a bad idea. We're kids in a kid world. This investigator is a grown-up. She's probably used to dealing with big-time crimes, like stealing cars and . . . trains."

"Trains?" asked Lydia.

"I couldn't think of anything bigger than cars. Except houses. But I don't think anyone steals houses."

"The getaway would be hard," Lydia agreed.

"Anyway, you know what I'm saying," said Armin.

Micah sighed. "I just have to know what's going on. Something doesn't smell right, and I've got to know what it is."

Lydia frowned and started tapping her foot. "Fine," she said finally. "Whatever. But if it turns out Tre's some kind of supervillain, and he figures out you're hot on his trail, don't count on me to bail you out of his secret lair."

"You're kidding, right?" Micah asked.

"I guess we'll find out."

Angel McManus's private investigator's office did not look anything like Micah had expected. Judging from the impressively large billboard that was nearly as wide as the entire Gas & Save, he would have guessed she had a classy office in some high-rise building in a fancy part of town.

He should have known better. Mostly because Middletown didn't have any high-rise buildings. Or fancy parts of town. Not to mention, that the office was even open on a Saturday should have told him something.

The detective's office was only three blocks from the food truck. Despite it being in a less-than-fancy part of town, Micah had to admit that proximity to the food truck would make it a pretty cool place to work! It was a two-room office on the second floor, just above the "Smells Fresh" Dry Cleaners and right next door to the Toilet Plunger Emporium.

He walked up the stairs and into a small lobby. There was a fake palm tree in one corner, and a fluorescent light buzzed from the ceiling. On the wall next to the door to Ms. McManus's office was a huge poster of Maxx Dryver standing in front of a sunset, with his arms crossed. The words "No Dirtballs Allowed!" were written in big, white letters across the bottom of the picture.

Maxx was Micah's favorite TV cop, and "No dirtballs allowed" was one of his best catchphrases. Micah smiled and nodded. With a poster like that, McManus had to be awesome at her job!

The door to Ms. McManus's office was closed, but Micah could hear a man's voice coming from inside. In fact, the voice sounded weirdly familiar. Where had he heard it before? Was it somebody famous? Someone he'd heard on the radio or TV?

Micah heard the door open and looked up to see Ms. McManus holding it for someone who was on his way out. The man behind her spoke softly, but the lobby was quiet other than the softly buzzing light, so Micah could hear every word he said.

" . . . just a tiny comb specifically for combing

mustaches. It was right there in my desk; then suddenly it was gone!"

"I'll do my best, Mr. Turtell. I'll call you if I have anything to report."

Mr. Turtell caught Micah's eye as he was putting on his coat. "I don't usually . . . ," he mumbled to Micah. "It's just . . . I . . . er . . . um . . . well . . . never mind."

Micah nodded. He couldn't help but feel exactly the same way.

As Mr. Turtell headed out the front door, Ms. McManus held her office door open for Micah.

"Next," she said.

Her voice was nothing like her first name would suggest. It was all rough and grindy, like if you accidentally tried to shove a mechanical pencil into an electric pencil sharpener. (Not that Micah had ever tried anything like that before.) She looked like the picture on the billboard, but maybe ten years older and a whole lot scarier. Her expression said she'd send her own grandma to jail if she found any dirt on her.

She started right in. "So, what's the story? Who are you trying to get in trouble? Your wife? Your boss? Your landlord?"

"I'm too young to have any of those things," said Micah.

Angel squinted her eyes and looked him up and down. "Sure. Whatever. Have it your way. So, what are you here for, then?"

"Well, . . ." Micah paused, then decided to just go for it.

"There's a new kid at school, and I think there's something fishy about him. Like he's hiding something."

"You're probably right. Almost everybody's hiding something." Angel looked from side to side as if she was about to tell him an important secret. Then her voice got softer. "So, what, exactly, are you looking to get out of this? What's your endgame here? You want him locked up for life? Kicked out of the country? What?"

"No! Of course not! Nothing like that!" Micah hadn't expected it to go this direction. "I just thought, you know, that maybe you could do some investigating and see if he has any dark secrets in his past. Something he's trying to hide."

"So you can blackmail him?"

Now Micah was having serious second thoughts. Maybe Lydia and Armin were right. Maybe this was a really bad idea. He stood up to go. "I think I've got to get home. I'm late for . . . stuff."

He was terrible at making excuses.

"Just leave the kid's name and age, and I'll take care of the rest," said Angel.

"No . . . that's okay. Maybe I'll come back and do that another time."

"The first investigation's on me. Trust me, I do great work!"

"I really should be going."

"I can make it so you never have to see him again!"

What!?! Did she really just say that? What kind of a place was this? But Micah tried to act as casual as possible. He certainly didn't want to get on her bad side. "Um . . . I'm gonna go. My mom will be worried if I don't get home soon."

Micah darted through the door and closed it behind him before she could get another word in.

There had to be another way to figure out what was up with Tre. But from now on, he'd be sure to only go to kids for help!

Because, wow! The adult world was terrifying! He was so glad he didn't have a wife or a boss or a landlord yet.

Alone

Looks like I'm on my own to seek out the truth about Tre. Armin and Lydia just don't see it. They are too blinded by his bright smile, I guess.

I definitely don't want help from Ms. McManus, our local private investigator. My visit with her gave me the creeps!

I just wish everyone would look at this situation more clearly. Sure, he's nice and all. But we've made this guy into some sort of hero before knowing all there is to know about him.

There's got to be more to this kid. And I'm determined to find it out before I let him in any further . . . even if I have to do it alone.

If you need wisdom, ask our generous God, and he will give it to you.
James 1:5 (NLT)

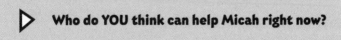

▷ **What do YOU do or who do you turn to when you feel alone?**

▷ **Who do YOU think can help Micah right now?**

CHAPTER SEVEN

It was Monday morning once again. How was there another Monday already? Micah could've sworn they were coming faster than once a week these days, although he had no idea how the authorities were pulling it off.

Mr. Turtell had not yet looked up from his desk as kids rolled into the classroom and sat down. Micah was wondering if it was going to be awkward between them, since over the weekend they'd seen each other outside of school. That was weird enough on its own, not to mention the fact that it was at a private investigator's office.

At last Mr. Turtell looked up from his desk and glanced around the room to see which kids were present and which to mark absent. Luckily, there was nothing particularly strange about the way he looked at Micah when he got to his row. But Micah did notice his mustache looked a bit untidy.

Mr. Turtell stood up to address his students. "As you know, right now we're studying America's expansion into the west. And, as luck would have it, we have a real, live Californian right here in our classroom! What are the chances?"

Katie raised her hand. "Who are you talking about, Mr. Turtell?"

"Tre, of course. He's from LA."

"I thought you said he was from California. That's where Californians are from, right?"

"Yes. That's right. Californians are from California. But LA is *in California*."

"Oh."

Mr. Turtell took a deep breath. "As I was saying, we have a Californian in our midst who also happens to be an excellent student. So, I thought we could take advantage of the situation and ask him a few questions. I'm sure he has some wonderful insights into the culture, climate, and topography of California and how that has affected the socioeconomic development of the region."

"How the what has affected the what now?" Micah whispered to Lydia.

"That's just a fancy way of saying, 'What's California like?'" Lydia answered.

"Oh."

Mr. Turtell looked over at Tre. "Mr. Buzznik, would you mind coming to the front of the class and fielding a few questions."

If it were Micah, this would have been torture, but Tre seemed to take it all in stride. "Sure, Mr. Turtell."

He casually strutted up to the front of the class and sat down on a stool the teacher had pulled out for him.

"So," said Mr. Turtell, "who has a question for Tre?"

Almost every hand in the room shot up. To

Micah's surprise, one of those hands belonged to Chet. Tre nodded at him to ask his question.

"So, if you're from California, do you think you're better than us?"

"Oh my!" Lydia whispered to Micah as she held her head in her hands. "How's he supposed to answer a question like that?"

Micah, meanwhile, thought Chet had a valid point. Did Tre think he was better than them? What would he say??

Tre paused, looking off into the distance. "Like . . . no."

Chet nodded. "Good answer."

"Thank you, Chet," Mr. Turtell said. "Who else has a question for Tre?"

Once again, almost every kid in the classroom raised their hand. In fact, Micah noticed that it actually *was* every kid in the classroom. Except him. What was up with everybody? Couldn't they tell a fake when they saw one? Tre probably wasn't even from California!

"Katie," said Mr. Turtell. "You have a question for Tre?"

Katie put her hand down and smiled from ear to ear. "Tre, your accent is *so* dreamy!"

"That's not a question," said Mr. Turtell.

"Oh. Sorry. I hadn't gotten there yet. Your accent is, like, really hard for me to imitate. So, I was wondering: did you have to learn how to talk like that right away when you were a baby, or did they teach it to you later when you'd already been talking for a few years?"

Tre looked at her, baffled. "That's totally not how accents work, dude. You have an accent too,

126

you know. From Middletown. I just happen to have, like, a California one. I didn't have to learn it—it's just the way I talk. Know what I mean?"

Katie nodded, as if it was all clear to her now. Micah doubted that this was true. Things were rarely clear to Katie.

Meanwhile, the look on Mr. Turtell's face told him that this question-and-answer time was not going exactly as he'd planned.

"Okay, just a few more questions. Liam?"

Liam stood up, almost like he was about to give a speech of his own. "You're from California, right, Tre? Which is really big. But our state is just regular-sized. So, do you ever feel cramped here, like you don't have enough space?"

"Umm . . . ," Tre started, looking bewildered. "I don't think I understand what you mean."

"I mean, do you ever feel like you don't have enough room for all your stuff?"

"No, I've got enough room for my stuff."

"That's good."

Mr. Turtell tried to maintain order, choosing students with their hands up. But now everyone was too excited to pay attention to their teacher.

"The gold rush was in California, right?" asked Makayla. "So, are you rich?"

"That's not an appropriate question, Makayla!" said Mr. Turtell.

"Sorry," Makayla apologized. "What I meant to say was, do you have a lot of money?"

Tre was starting to look a little less chill than usual. His chill factor had definitely changed. On a scale of not chill to max chill, Tre was in dangerously not chill territory. A small part of Micah felt sorry for him. Whether he was keeping secrets or not, he hadn't asked to be bombarded with questions.

Mr. Turtell must have noticed the same thing. He sighed. "Okay, Tre. You can sit down now."

"Thanks, Mr. Turtell," said Tre.

Mr. Turtell smiled weakly. "And thank you, class, for all your . . . um . . . insightful questions."

Next Mr. Turtell asked the class to do some silent

reading from their history books. Micah was pretty sure this was his way of taking a little break in order to keep what was left of his sanity. Fifteen minutes into their reading, the intercom clicked on and Mr. Drury's voice came through.

"Mr. Turtell, could you send Tre to the office? It's time for him to do an interview on the PB and J show."

Of course, Mr. Drury. Tre?"

"Oh yeah," Tre said. "I forgot I'd agreed to do that."

By the look on Tre's face, Micah could tell he wasn't too excited about it.

This time Micah poked Lydia on the shoulder. "Tre doesn't seem to want PB and J to interview him. Which is exactly how you'd react if you had something to hide!"

Lydia stared at him and shook her head. "It's also how you'd react if you'd just been asked a bunch of ridiculous questions and weren't looking forward to another round."

Micah shrugged. She may have had a point.

Fifteen minutes later, Mr. Turtell turned on the classroom TV. It was time for *The PB and J Report*. The best (and only) celebrity news show at New Leaf Elementary.

"Welcome to *The PB and J Report*!" said PB. "Where we take you to the stars—"

"—and bring the stars to you!" finished J.

"Today we're honored to have a special guest fifth grader on our program who has starred in movies, television, and even commercials!"

"Even commercials?" asked J. "How cool is that!"

"How cool indeed, J," said PB. "We're thrilled to welcome New Leaf's own, Tre Buzznik!"

The camera panned to a smiling Tre.

In Micah's classroom, Makayla screamed. "Look! Tre's on TV! He's really on TV!"

"I know him! I totally know him!" Katie yelled.

"He sits right in front of me in class!" shouted Mara.

"I think we all knew that," said Micah. "Since this is the class you're talking about. And he just walked out of here."

Mara gave Micah a dirty look. "Whatever."

Back on the TV, J was asking Tre a question. "So, what big project are you working on these days? A TV show? A movie? A commercial?"

"Right now I'm working on an awesome independent film. It's got elves and hunchbacks and heroes and monsters and sword fights!"

"That sounds incredible!" said PB. "What's the movie called?"

"Actually . . ." Tre paused. "Come to think of it, I'm not sure it has a name yet."

"That's weird, don't you think, PB?"

"Indeed it is, J! So, who's the director? Is it someone we've heard of?"

Tre nodded. "Probably. It's Micah."

"Micah who?" J. asked.

"Micah Murphy. From Mr. Turtell's fifth-grade class."

"Huh," said PB, looking disappointed. "I've never heard of him."

Back in the classroom, Micah shook his head.

"Are you kidding me? I've talked to PB and J at least, like, twenty times." He said this out loud to no one in particular.

Once again, no one in particular listened to him.

Meanwhile, Tre continued talking on the TV. "Micah's my friend, and he's awesome. He's a super-talented director and writer. The movie's got a wonderful cast. His sister's in the movie too, along with Lydia, and Armin, and Gabe."

"Hey, that's me!" Armin, Lydia, and Gabe shouted all at once.

Meanwhile, Micah wasn't interested in being recognized anymore. He was too busy thinking. A certain part of him was proud—proud his movie was being talked about on TV. (even if it was just on an elementary school program), and proud that Tre thought he was a talented writer and director.

But he wasn't sure what to do with Tre calling him a friend. *Were* they friends? Micah had always had three friends—Lydia, Armin, and Gabe. Did he have room for a fourth? Would that mess with his friendships with the others?

He looked over at Armin, Lydia, and Gabe. They seemed completely unfazed by Tre calling him a friend.

Micah, on the other hand, was completely fazed by it. Meanwhile, PB and J were still talking to Tre.

"Well, that sounds amazing!" said PB.

"Yeah," said J. "I love movies with monsters and elves and stuff!"

PB was making his thinking face. "Wait a second. Is Micah Murphy that normal-sized kid with normal brown hair and a normal-looking face?"

"Umm . . . yeah, I guess so."

"Oh yeah! I remember him," said PB. Then he paused, looking at Tre questioningly. "But the guy I'm thinking of doesn't have any talent."

Armin patted Micah on the back. "Well, at least they remember who you are now!"

Micah sighed and wondered if he could go back to being forgotten.

At lunchtime that day, Tre sat with Micah and his friends. Micah hadn't remembered to pack a lunch from home, and the cafeteria was serving up a sardine egg bake. As he used his plastic fork to break through the crusty top layer of fish and mozzarella cheese, Micah tried to talk himself into accepting Tre into his friendship circle.

After all, there were good things about having Tre as a friend. Because of *The PB and J Report*, everyone was swarming all around their table. They were now cool by association! In fact, there were so many people around, asking questions and chatting them up, it was hard to get a word in edgewise.

Katie was the first to come over.

"Hey Tre! I saw you on TV today! If you need a damsel in distress for your movie, just say the word!"

She smiled her prettiest smile. "You could totally rescue me anytime you want!"

"Well," Tre began, "that's not really up to me. Micah here is the writer and director, so he's, like, in charge of those decisions."

Tre looked at Micah. Katie did not.

"Okay,". Katie said to Tre. "Just let me know if you change your mind."

Micah sighed. Maybe he and his friends weren't cool by association after all. Tre seemed to be keeping the attention all to himself.

Katie walked away. But just as Tre took a bite of egg bake, Hanz appeared at his side. "I assume you know zat my family is also in ze movie business."

Tre glanced at Micah and shared a surprised look with him. "I didn't know that, Hanz."

"Ah yes. My uncle is ze big-time movie producer. His films are huge in eastern Europe. I'm sure you heard of ze box office smash hit *The Latvian Enforcer*?"

"No, I don't think so."

"Hmm . . . How about *All Roads Lead to Estonia*?"

"Umm . . . that movie doesn't sound familiar either."

Hanz shrugged. "Zat is your loss. But perhaps our paths vill cross in Hollywood sometime, on ze set of one of his enormous blockbusting hits."

"Perhaps," said Tre.

But there was no time to ponder the weirdness of that conversation. Because now Chet was at Tre's side. His arms were crossed, and he nodded at him with a gruff look on his face. "You're pretty famous, huh?"

"I wouldn't say that, bruh. Why do you ask?"

"I was thinking you might need a bodyguard."

"Not at the moment."

Chet nodded. Then his eyes darted left and right. "Just so you know, I can have people removed."

"Removed?" Tre asked.

Chet nodded. "You just say the word, and it's done."

Micah thought back to his weird encounter with

the private investigator. Maybe the kid world was just as scary as the grown-up world after all!

Tre nodded back at Chet. "Okay. Thanks, I guess."

As Chet walked away, Tre glanced at Micah and shrugged.

But by the time they both turned around again, Micah started to wonder if maybe they'd sent Chet away too quickly. Maybe Tre really did need a bodyguard! The line to talk to him now included almost everybody in the room. Autograph seekers and well-wishers were stretched all the way back to the milk refrigerator at the end of the lunch line!

"Tre, could you sign my T-shirt?" asked Jose.

"Could you sign my binder?" asked Gabby.

"Could you sign my pencil?" asked Roberto.

"Sure," said Tre.

"Do you know any famous people? Maybe Chris Hallsworth?" asked Tommy.

"No."

"Do you know Chris Pruitt?" asked Deepali.

"No."

"Do you know Jennifer Logan?" asked Magnus.

"No."

"Do you know Spider-Man?" asked Gabe.

"Spider-Man's not a real person," said Tre.

"So then, no?"

"Sorry. No."

Tre looked exhausted. Micah was beginning to think being popular was overrated. Was that possible? It seemed unlikely.

Friends?

I don't get it. Why would Tre call me his friend? We barely know each other! True, I've let him in on my movie, but that doesn't make us friends.

Once again, this guy is messing with my life in a big way. I've already got friends. Good ones, too. Friends I know everything about. Friends who are just as average as I am (okay, maybe Armin and Lydia are a bit above average, but Gabe balances us all out).

Is Tre my friend? And if he is my friend, should I be this suspicious of him?

Do not copy the behavior and customs of this world, but let God [change] the way you think. Then you will learn to know God's will for you, which is good.
Romans 12:2 (NLT)

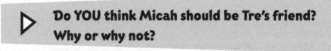

▷ **Do YOU think Micah should be Tre's friend? Why or why not?**

▷ **How can YOU let God change the way you think about friendships?**

CHAPTER EIGHT

It was recess a few days later, and Chet was chasing Micah across the playground. That probably doesn't sound all that surprising—when you're a fifth-grade boy at recess, chasing is just what you do. All in good fun, right?

Wrong.

This was not good fun at all.

Chet wasn't chasing Micah so he could tag him, shout "You're it," and then run away laughing. He was chasing Micah so he could pummel him into a pile of mush on the sidewalk. Why did Chet want to pummel Micah into a pile of mush on the sidewalk?

It might have been simply that Micah was Micah and Chet was Chet, so this was the natural order of things. Chet was a bully, and pummeling people into mush is the sort of thing bullies enjoy.

On the other hand, there was a slight possibility it was because of the dissected worm Micah had tossed onto Chet's face, where it stuck to his upper lip like a mustache.

Yes. That was probably it.

It had happened by accident (not that this mattered to Chet). Everyone in class had been happily cutting open dead worms in Mr. Beaker's science lab to see all their organs. It was awesome! Micah had no idea worms were so cool and complicated on the inside.

At the end of class, they were tidying up—washing worm guts and whatnot off their hands—when Micah noticed a ruler leaning at an angle against the edge of the tray that his worm was pinned to.

"Look, Armin. It's like a catapult."

Armin smiled. "You should put something small

on the end of it and try to launch it into that trash can over there."

"Brilliant!" said Micah. "That way we can clean up our area and have fun all at the same time!"

They flicked several wadded-up paper towels into the trash, and then a couple of binder clips and some pieces of notebook paper that had gotten worm juice on them. There were more misses than hits, but eventually they launched everything into the can.

"Are we all cleaned up now?" Armin asked, glancing around.

"Yep, except for the worm we were dissecting, still pinned to the tray."

"Are we supposed to throw that away too?"

"I guess so. I'm sure my mom doesn't want me to bring it home."

"But we shouldn't try to catapult it, should we?" Armin asked.

"Probably not. But . . . maybe? What do you think? It sure would be fun to try."

"Maybe just one try," said Armin. "If we don't get it in the trash on the first shot, we'll call it quits."

"That sounds smart," said Micah.

But it was not smart at all. One try was one too many.

Armin let Micah have the honor, and Micah placed the worm on the end of the catapult. He hit the other end of the ruler so that the end with the worm popped up in the air.

Fortunately, the worm stuck to the end of the ruler. That should have been the end of it. It was not.

"That didn't count, right?" asked Micah. "I mean, it didn't even launch into the air!"

"Of course it didn't count! You just need to hit it harder this time."

"Sounds smart," said Micah.

Once again, it was not.

Bam! Micah hit the ruler.

Whoosh! The dissected worm flew through the air this time.

Splat! The disemboweled worm smacked against Chet's upper lip, where it stuck like well-cooked spaghetti to a wall.

In hindsight, Micah should have immediately said, "I'm so sorry. I didn't mean to do that!" And there were half a dozen other things that would have been worth saying as well. But he didn't say any of them. Instead, he did something much, much worse.

He laughed.

The good news was, everyone else in the class agreed it was hilarious. The bad news was, no one else in the class laughed out loud. Because, after all, Chet is Chet. Nobody laughs at Chet and gets away with it.

Things I Should Have Said to Chet Instead of Laughing

- "That's a great fake mustache! The authorities will never catch you now."

- "The brown worm really brings out the color in your eyes."

- "I thought you looked hungry, and worms are a great source of protein!"

- "Wow! I didn't know they could jump like that! Especially after they're dead!"

- "Sorry. I was aiming at Hanz."

At the end of science, Chet told Micah he'd get him back at recess. Which was why he was now chasing Micah around the playground, getting ready to pummel him into something that vaguely resembled the worm guts that had splattered across his face.

Around and around the playground they ran, dodging the swings, circling the climbing wall, hurdling the teeter totters, weaving in and out of kindergartners. Micah had never run through an obstacle course that fast in his life. In fact, for a moment he thought he might be losing him, but when he turned around, Chet was still hot on his trail. This shouldn't have been surprising—after all, catching and squashing kids was what Chet did full-time.

For a moment Micah managed to catch his breath behind an oak tree, and he thought he might stay out of Chet's clutches until the bell rang. But alas, Chet spotted him, and he had to sprint away once again.

In and out, up and down, back and forth they ran. Micah knew the clock was ticking down and the bell couldn't wait much longer. How much more time was there, anyway? Maybe a couple minutes? If he could keep ahead of Chet just a little bit longer—

Bam!

Micah tripped over a tree root and landed on his face.

Well, that was it. He was about to have one hundred and fifty pounds of bully walloping him into the ground.

Micah braced himself.

Any moment now.

What was taking him so long?

Finally, Micah glanced behind him. Tre was there, just a few feet away, standing between himself and Chet. His hand was held out like a cop directing traffic at a busy intersection.

"You don't really want to hurt him, do ya, bruh?" Tre asked.

"Obviously!" Chet said with a shrug. "It's what I do. What kind of self-respecting bully would I be if I let kids get away with throwing worms at me? It's my duty to pound him!"

"Yeah, but you'll totally get in big trouble if you beat him up in front of all these people," said Tre.

"Whatever. I'm in trouble all the time anyway.

What difference does a little extra trouble make?"

"What if he tells you he's sorry? Would you forgive him then?"

"Ha!" From Chet, this was more of a shout than a laugh. "What difference would that make? I'd still have the taste of dead worm on my upper lip."

Ewww. Micah hadn't thought of that.

Tre didn't say anything for a moment, maybe thinking up the perfect strategy. Micah was unimpressed with where he landed: "How about you don't beat him up as a personal favor to me?" Tre asked.

Chet crossed his arms and squinted at him. "Why do you care, anyway?"

"He's my friend," Tre said. "I don't want to see him get pummeled."

How ridiculous, thought Micah. Asking for a favor from Chet would never work in a million years. Didn't this kid know anything?

"Yeah, okay," Chet said. "For you."

Then he walked away.

Wait! What just happened? Micah couldn't believe it! Tre had actually talked him down. How cool was this kid, anyway? Nobody'd ever talked Chet down from anything in his life!

Tre held a hand out to Micah, and Micah took it, pulling himself up off the ground.

"Thanks a lot!" Micah said. "I sure do appreciate that."

Tre shrugged. "No problem, bruh. That's what friends are for."

There was that word again. Oh well. He might as well get used to it.

When Micah got home that afternoon, he had some important research to do. "Dad, can I use the computer in the living room? I want to check out some stuff on YouTube for my movie."

"No problem. But don't get too distracted. Or you won't have any screen time left for video games."

Micah knew his dad was teasing him. But he wasn't wrong. Micah needed to focus if he was going to still have some video game time that night. After all, the Ptera-Vandals of *Captain Karate Dino Cop 4* weren't going to arrest themselves!

The reason Micah wanted to get on YouTube was to check out some of the things Tre was teaching them about sword fighting. Micah was coming around to the fact that Tre really was a pretty good guy. But could he possibly know as much as he pretended to? It still felt a little too good to be true.

So, he started looking things up.

Micah began with Eastern Deluvian freestyle fencing. Check. It was real. And judging from the two-minute video demonstration he found, it was awesome!

Highlander twist: check.

Spanish fist bump: check.

Allemande left: check. (It was also a square-dancing move, as he'd suspected. But additionally, it was an amazing sword spinning move that was perfect for countering the Spanish fist bump!)

Huh. So, Tre was cool, nice, *and* knowledgeable. Micah didn't know what to do with all that.

It wasn't long before a completely unrelated video caught his eye. This, Micah realized, was both the beauty and the curse of YouTube—it was way too easy to get distracted. Especially for fifth-grade boys, who were particularly distractible. What was he supposed to be doing again?

Robo Pirate action figures! He had no idea they even made those! And a cartoon to go with them!?!

Micah couldn't help but click on it, and quickly burned through five minutes of awesome mechanical pirates pummeling droid villains. But then a short commercial came on the screen, interrupting his Robo Pirate cartoon.

Wait! That was weird. Why would this show have a commercial for something that was just for toddlers? Was *Robo Pirates* a cartoon for babies? And if so, why did they make it so awesome? It was so hard to tell who the audience for stuff was these days.

As Micah finished watching the commercial, he felt a rush of embarrassment pass over him, and he was just about to click off the screen, when all of a sudden, he saw something that looked unbelievably familiar.

The toddler in the commercial. That smile. Those dimples. That hair flip.

Was it possible? Could it really be Tre? And if so, why on earth was he in a commercial for . . .

Hug 'ems Tug 'ems Diapers?!?

The Secret's Out

Hug 'ems Tug 'ems Diapers?! Is Tre's big film career just . . . a diaper commercial?! How embarrassing! Pfft! Some big movie star he turned out to be!

Come to think of it, he's never mentioned any roles he's played. I can't blame him. Who would brag about being in a diaper commercial?

It may not even be him. But that little guy in a diaper sure does look like Tre.

Hmmm . . .

A gossip goes around revealing a secret, but a trustworthy person keeps a confidence. Proverbs 11:13 (CSB)

▷ **What do YOU think Micah should do with this discovery?**

▷ **What would YOU do if you found out something embarrassing about your friend?**

CHAPTER NINE

There he was, dancing around, so proud of himself for not wetting the bed that night. Micah watched in shock as the toddler-sized Tre declared: "I've got a full diaper, Mom, Mom.

This was so humiliating! Micah couldn't imagine what it must be like for Tre to live with a secret like this. What could be more embarrassing than being in a diaper commercial? Micah couldn't stop watching it over and over again. The jingle was actually kind of catchy:

I can pull my diaper up by myself
The stretchy waistband feels just right

Grab a new Hug 'ems off my shelf
And my sheets stay dry all night!

So, it turned out Micah had been right all along, Tre really did have something to hide! If his secret life as a diaper model got out, it would be the end of his popularity forever! He'd be a laughingstock. They'd call him names like the Tug 'ems Turd or Diaper Dude or something even more clever (which Micah couldn't wait to think up later)!

This was amazing! Or terrible. What did he want for Tre again? Were they friends? Or was this the beginning of the end for the new kid?

How well did Micah even really know him? Could this be the reason Tre hadn't shown anyone his acting work? If he was keeping a secret like this, what else was he hiding?

Wait a second! This was ridiculous! There was no way Micah could be sure it was really Tre as a toddler. I mean, sure, the dimples and hair and everything looked just like him, but that didn't mean anything. It was too long ago for him to be certain. After all, the commercial had to have been recorded, like, seven or eight years ago, right?

He looked at the video again. Hug 'ems, Inc. 5,243 likes. Published five years ago.

Say what?! Did he read that right? If he'd done the math, that would have made Tre . . . (pause to count on fingers) five. He was five when he was in a diaper commercial?!

That made it even more embarrassing! It's one thing to be a bed-wetter for all the world to see when you were a toddler. But a kindergartner?

Aha! I knew he was hiding something, Micah thought. *He thinks he can win everyone over with his cool accent and hair. I'll show them who he really is. Then maybe my life will go back to normal!*

Micah took a deep breath. *Okay. Take a moment to think this through.* What was he supposed to do now? Should he share this commercial with the world? Confront Tre with what he'd learned?

He was getting ahead of himself. What he needed to do first was make sure it was really Tre. But how?

Who had the computer skills to uncover somebody's well-hidden past, but could also keep it a secret and wouldn't think Micah was crazy?

In a flash of brilliance, the answer came to him.

Rachel Dershwitz was the best technology whiz in the fifth grade. She was also a huge conspiracy theorist. In fact, Micah had had to learn what the words "conspiracy theorist" even meant because of her. Lydia, the vocabulary queen, called her that once, and then had to explain it to Micah. A conspiracy theorist was someone who believed *everyone* was hiding something— the government, teachers, scientists, parents, mall Santas, etc. In other words, all of society's most powerful people!

Rachel didn't trust anyone older than twelve and was always looking over her shoulder and saying things like "They're watching our every move!" and "That's what *they* want you to believe!" (Micah had asked her who "they" were once. She just tut-tutted and said, "If you don't know, then they've already won!" He never asked again.)

It had been raining all Tuesday morning, which meant indoor recess. Usually this was one of the worst things that could happen to a fifth- grade boy, but today Micah didn't mind. It would make it all the easier to find Rachel and have a chat with her.

A Few of Rachel's Favorite Conspiracies

- To keep kids under control, the government puts tracking devices in school lunches. That's why the grapes in fruit cups never really taste like grapes.

- Bigfoot is a super soldier the military cloned for cold weather missions.

- Top secret international spies use secret codes on math tests to pass information to agents embedded in the school system.

- The moon landing never happened. Apollo 11 actually landed on an alien spacecraft to negotiate a treaty. To keep the peace, it cost Earth twelve hundred boxes of Cocoa Krispies and a ring-tailed lemur. Some believe it was too high a price to pay.

- All cats are Russian spies.

During almost every indoor recess, Rachel could be found at Mr. Turtell's computer.

"What are you doing today?" Micah asked her.

"Mr. Turtell's taxes."

"Are you kidding me? He trusts you with his taxes?"

"I know where all the loopholes in the tax code are."

Micah didn't know what a loophole was, but it sounded like the sort of thing she'd know where to find.

"I was wondering if I could talk to you about something," Micah said.

"You already are."

"I meant something else."

"Go for it. As long as I don't have to look up from what I'm doing."

That seemed about right. He got closer to her ear and whispered. "I wanted to ask if you'd be willing to look into something private for me."

"Could you be more specific?"

"I want you to investigate Tre's past."

"Tre Buzznik? He's cool."

Micah sighed. "Yeah, I know. Everybody thinks so. And I'm not saying he's not. He's actually a friend of mine."

"Then why do you want me digging into his past?"

"Because I found something I think he's hiding. It's an old video. But I want to make sure it's really him before I talk to him about it."

"So, what's in it for me?"

"What do you want?"

She didn't even pause to think about it. "Fourteen paper clips, seven rubber bands, and nine tater tots."

This was not what Micah had expected. "What do you need all that stuff for?"

"I'm going to use the paper clips and rubber bands to set up an interference system around my computer, which will flip the connectivity code and allow a workaround to circumvent the IMP traps."

"Um . . . circumwhat the what, now?"

"It's so the government can't spy on my personal computer system."

"Good move. And why do you want the tater tots?"

"Because tater tots are awesome."

True enough.

Rachel finally looked up from what she was doing on Mr. Turtell's computer. "I want the paper clips and rubber bands up front, and then you can give me the tots when I give you the information."

"Okay," said Micah. "Consider it done."

Two days later, on Thursday morning, it was time for the drop-off. The sky was battleship gray, and a chill wind blew through Micah's coat. Rachel told him to meet her at a park bench two blocks from New Leaf Elementary, fifteen minutes before the school day began. When he arrived, she was already there waiting for him, her head wrapped so tightly in a scarf and hat, he could only see her eyes. He sat down beside her.

"Why did we have to meet so early?" Micah asked.

"This isn't early," Rachel said. "When do you usually get to school?"

"Right when it starts," Micah answered.

"Oh. That figures. I always show up everywhere at least ten minutes early so I can scope things out. I don't want any surprises waiting for me."

"Sheesh," said Micah. "Being a conspiracy theorist sounds exhausting."

"You have no idea."

She handed him a heavy grocery bag.

"I did a deep dive into the history of your 'friend'."

Micah could hear the sarcasm in her voice as she said the word "friend." But he probably deserved it.

She went on. "In this bag you'll find a thorough binder detailing all of Tre's activities."

Micah glanced inside the bag. He was surprised. "Why a binder? I expected you'd give me the information electronically—maybe in an email or a flash drive or something."

"Are you kidding me?" Rachel asked. "If I sent you an email or saved it in a file, there would be a digital footprint. Then everything I did could be hacked and traced back to me. That's exactly what 'the Man' wants me to do."

"Sorry. Makes sense, I guess. Which man wants you to do this again?"

"Oh, never mind." She sighed and stood up from the bench. "Anyway, everything you ever wanted to know about him is in there."

"And how about you? Are you going to keep this between us?"

"You can do with this information whatever you want, but I won't let anyone know what I found out. I don't squeal on private citizens. I only rat out government agencies and corporate conglomerates."

Micah didn't know what a corporate conglomerate was, but agreed they probably needed ratting out. "Umm . . . okay."

"So, you got my tots?" Rachel asked.

Micah handed her a ziplock bag. "I warmed them up for you in the toaster oven this morning."

"Thanks," Rachel said. "That was thoughtful."

She smiled. Micah had never seen Rachel smile before. It was nicer than he'd expected. Weird, but nice.

As Rachel walked away, Micah took the binder out of the bag and began flipping through it. Fascinating! Or not, actually. The fascinating part was that Tre had actually lived a pretty boring life.

Some of the backstory Tre had told on his first day checked out. He was born in LA, where he lived until he was eight. Then he moved to San Diego and then finally landed in Middletown. But his real name wasn't even Tre Buzznik! It was Trestorian Ledorkenson! How . . . *dorky*!

And he'd completely made up the stuff about being on TV and in movies. Actually, it looks more like his dad had been on TV. *Interesting*, Micah thought. *I wonder if I've seen his dad in anything . . .*

Somehow Rachel had found a bunch of small acting parts Tre had tried out for. Probably trying to follow in his father's footsteps. But Tre hadn't actually gotten any of them! He'd auditioned for a time-traveling western musical (awesome!), a space drama about werewolves (amazing!), and a TV public service announcement that taught kids the dangers of double-dipping their nachos (heartbreaking). But someone else had landed every part.

But then, buried deep in the binder, on the bottom of page 237, Micah saw it. When Tre was five and a half years old, he actually did land one part: a commercial for Hug 'ems Tug 'ems Diapers! There were several pictures of Tre on the set in his diaper. He had a baby face when he was in kindergarten, which was clearly how he'd gotten the part. Not to mention the fact that he was perfectly on pitch when he sang the Hug 'ems jingle, which would not have been an easy feat for an actual toddler.

But why would he try out for the part in the first place? And why would his parents have let him? Surely they knew what this would mean for his future? The scar it would leave on his reputation?

Or maybe they didn't. Maybe they just thought it was a fun job, and they had no idea how mean kids could be if they found out about it. Wow. How naive of them!

Micah glanced down at his watch. Nuts. He was late for school.

He'd clearly make a terrible conspiracy theorist.

The Truth Stinks

It's true . . . Tre was in a diaper commercial . . . when he was five years old! It's actually kind of sad . . . and humiliating. And infuriating!

How could this guy walk around like some movie star while he's hiding a secret like this? If he lied about his "acting career," what else is he hiding? What exactly can we believe about Tre?

I need to confront him, tear down the facade he's so carefully built, and reveal the truth. It's the right thing to do . . . right? My friends are being fooled by him, and the lies need to stop. Now!

Don't betray another person's secret.
Proverbs 25:9 (NLT)

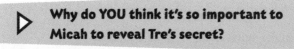

▷ Why do YOU think it's so important to Micah to reveal Tre's secret?

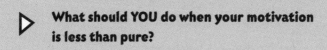

▷ What should YOU do when your motivation is less than pure?

CHAPTER TEN

On Friday morning, Micah woke up exhausted. He'd been so angry after finding out the truth about Tre's past the night before that he couldn't sleep. How could Tre hide who he really was while playing the part of Micah's friend? (Which he did a really good job of, by the way.) The new kid had everyone fooled! Micah would have been fooled himself, if he hadn't been watching Tre so closely.

On his way to school, Micah found himself hiding behind a bush, waiting for Tre to walk past. He knew Tre's route and that he walked to school by himself, so it would be the perfect time to catch him alone and have a heart-to-heart chat.

Micah had tossed and turned all night, wondering what he should do. Should he tell the whole school about the real Tre? Or talk to Tre about it privately? Or just forget about it until Tre brought it up, if he ever did?

After thinking it over for a long time, Micah decided it was important for Tre's past to get out in the open for three reasons: One, he wanted everything to get back to normal with his friends. If they learned Tre wasn't as cool as they thought, then maybe they wouldn't pay so much attention to him anymore, and things would go back to the way things were before. They'd give Micah the respect he deserved for being in charge of his movie, and he wouldn't have to fight for his creative vision to be realized all the time! Movies couldn't handle more than one creative genius on the set!

Two, he loved being right! Nobody had believed him when he said Tre was hiding something. And what fun was it to be right if nobody else knew it? Didn't he deserve an "I told you so"?

And finally, three (and most important), didn't everybody have the right to know everything about everybody else? Wasn't that in the Constitution or something? He was pretty sure it was. So, it would be wrong for Micah *not* to share this information with the world . . . Right?

Now Micah was standing behind a bush on Clark Street, waiting for Tre to approach, probably with his skateboard under his arm.

"Hey Micah, what are you doing in that bush, bro?" Tre had snuck up beside him. Seriously?!

"Aha! Waiting to ambush you, that's what!" Micah was trying not to seem crushed that his sneak attack hadn't turned out quite like he had hoped. "I know all about your past, Tre."

"Huh? What past?"

"I've got a full diaper, Mom, Mom," Micah mimicked in his best toddler voice. But Tre didn't seem to get it.

Then, Micah started singing a few bars of the Hug 'ems jingle:

I can pull my diaper up by myself
The stretchy waistband feels just right
Grab a new Hug 'ems off my shelf
And my sheets stay dry all night!

Tre's face went pale. "What are you talking about? I don't know that song."

"I saw you on the commercial. I wasn't sure it was you at first, but Rachel Dershwitz traced it back online."

"Rachel who?" Tre's brow wrinkled.

"She does Mr. Turtell's taxes?" Micah tried to connect the dots.

"Doesn't help."

"I paid her with tater tots . . . Never mind."

A look of horror passed over Tre's face. "Please don't say anything! I don't want to go through this again!"

Micah smiled, knowing he had won. But winning didn't feel quite as good as he thought it would. "What are you talking about?" Micah asked.

"Yes. It's all true. I never should have taken the part! But my dad got me the gig because he's in the business. I had no idea what a big deal it would become. It turned me into a total doofus in LA! Everybody found out about it. They called me, "Tug 'em the Bed-Wetter." It was humiliating! It didn't matter what else I did, I would always just be, "Tug 'em," to them."

Tre shook his head. "I can't believe this is happening again! Moving to San Diego didn't help. When my parents moved us to Middletown, they tried to get rid of my past once and for all. They did their best to scrub the internet clean of all references to me in that commercial. My mom even bought me cool clothes and got me a cool haircut. I changed my name and my accent. I even carry around this stupid skateboard even though I don't know how to ride it!

"So, what are you going to do?" Tre asked. "Are you going to tell everybody?"

Micah nodded. "Absolutely! I'm going to make

a huge announcement on *The PB and J Report*! It's going to be awesome."

"For you," Tre muttered.

Of course. What else would Micah have meant?

Micah and his friends had another filming session after school that day. It was cold and bleak, and he was in a bad mood. They only had a handful more scenes to film, but he wasn't in a very creative or energetic place at the moment. He just wanted to get it over with.

"Where's Tre?" Armin asked.

"We're done filming his scenes," said Micah.

"But I thought he was coming anyway. I like how he does the makeup for my sword-fighting wounds."

"Yeah," said Gabe. "And I thought he was going to help me attach my hunch better. It keeps falling out of my cape when I roll down the hill in the final fight scene."

Micah ignored their questions. He wasn't surprised at all that Tre hadn't shown up. If it were him, he wouldn't have shown up either. So, it was just the four of them today: him, Gabe, Lydia, and Armin—oh yeah, and Barnabas. His sister, Audrey, wasn't there either, but nobody seemed bothered by that. They had enough tension and sarcasm without her.

"Armin and Gabe are right," Lydia said. "It's not the same without Tre. He contributes so much."

"We'll be fine," said Micah. "We've got this on our own. It's not like he was good at *everything* on a film set."

"Almost," said Armin under his breath.

But Micah heard it. He had to admit, he missed Tre too. Tre brought a true professionalism to the set. Everything just seemed to go better when he was around, and right now everyone seemed on the edge of breaking down.

Besides, even if he'd only been in one commercial, there was no denying Tre was an amazing actor. Every scene he was in was better because of him.

"Okay, let's forget about Tre for now," said Micah. "We've got to film the last few scenes. Lydia, is Barnabas in costume and makeup?"

"Does he look like he's in costume?" Lydia asked.

He did not. He just looked like a regular old dog. Not at all like a terrifying mer-dog, which was what the scene called for.

Micah shook his head. "Could somebody please help me tape on his Styrofoam dorsal fin?"

Lydia reluctantly came over to help. Micah sighed. It was going to be a long day of shooting.

The Many Roles of
Barnabas "Everydog" Murphy

Since Barnabas was the only animal I could rely on, I used him for all sorts of parts in my movie. Here's how me and my friends transformed Barnabas "Everydog" Murphy into eleven different roles!

- Mer-dog (Styrofoam dorsal fin and flippers make him look just like a fish!)

- Hunch-dog (we used a small fanny pack to get the proper effect)

- Pega-dog (coat hanger wires and cardboard make excellent wings)

- Swamp rats 1–6 (a long rat tail and pipe cleaner whiskers are all you really need–plus fancy camera work, to make it look like there are six of him)

- A three-headed dog who used to be mean but now is nice because he had two of his heads surgically removed (this just requires a couple of Band-aids–one on each side of the neck–so you can see where the heads were removed)

- Weird, hairy innkeeper who's always crawling around on his hands and knees, looking for spare change (requires no costume at all!)

Lydia sighed. "You know we still haven't landed on a title yet. When are you going to get around to that, Micah?"

"It's a lot of pressure," Micah admitted.

"I think we should call it *The Amazing Elf Princess*," Lydia announced.

"But the theme of the movie is about being true to who you are—and who you were destined to be," said Micah. "We need a title that truly captures the heart of the film. The journey and the struggle!"

Lydia rolled her eyes. "Fine. How about we call it, *We'll Fix It in Editing*."

"That's hilarious," said Micah, not meaning it at all. "How about we call it *The Bossy Elf Princess*."

Armin laughed.

"So, you think that's funny?" Lydia asked Armin. "Maybe we should go with *The Proud Warrior Who Was Scared of the Dark*."

"I think we should call it *The Last Hunchback*," said Gabe, not realizing they were trying to insult each other.

"But you're *not* the last hunchback," Micah corrected him. "Don't you remember in the second-to-last scene you discover your long-lost hunchback daughter, Requilda?"

"Oh yeah! That was awesome!" Gabe said. "So, let's call it *The Second to Last Hunchback.*"

Lydia blew out a long, exasperated breath, then said, "Or we could go with a really helpful title, like *A Hunchback Is Not a Whale.*"

Micah had to give her credit: she was doing a good job filling in for Audrey's missing sarcasm.

"I'm not sure *The Second to Last Hunchback* sets the right mood," Micah said to Gabe. "I want something that highlights all the amazing action scenes."

Gabe's eyes got wide, and he grinned from ear to ear. "How about *Duel Fight 2*?"

"Why 2?" asked Armin.

"Because that makes it twice as cool!"

The Weight of Truth

Well . . . I confronted Tre. I told him I knew all about his secret role in a diaper commercial. I don't care how embarrassed he is. That's no excuse for lying. Sure, I've done my fair share of lying, but this is different. He's made everyone believe he's the coolest kid around.

I guess technically Tre didn't lie . . . But he made everyone believe he was their friend. Friends don't keep secrets from each other like he did.

The thing is, confronting Tre didn't feel as good as I thought it would. Sounds like that commercial has followed him around most of his childhood. He sounded pretty crushed that I discovered the truth.

[Love] does not dishonor others, it is not self-seeking . . . It always protects.
1 Corinthians 13:5, 7 (NIV)

▷ **Why do YOU think Micah isn't as happy about confronting Tre as he thought he'd be?**

▷ **What do YOU think Micah's next move should be?**

CHAPTER ELEVEN

It was not a good weekend.

For weeks Micah had been excited about getting started on editing his movie. He'd spent hours learning all kinds of new editing techniques from YouTube videos, articles, and even honest-to-goodness books made of real paper and ink! It was amazing how much he'd learned, and he'd been waiting to put it all into practice with the film he'd made with his friends.

But all weekend long he just couldn't concentrate. Again and again his mind went back to Tre's secret. He was doing the right thing by making plans to announce it on *The PB and J Report*, right? He'd thought about it from every angle, and he kept coming to the same conclusion. So, why did his brain refuse to let him think about anything else? What was wrong with his brain, anyway?

If he asked Lydia, he was sure she'd have an answer or two (she was always questioning the workings of his brain), but he didn't want to tell his friends what he knew just yet. He was waiting for the big reveal.

Which was why Micah didn't have anyone to talk to about his brain troubles. Ugh!

Now it was Monday morning, and Micah was sitting in Mr. Turtell's class. He couldn't stop staring at the back of Tre's head, two rows in front of him.

"So, what's the big announcement?" Lydia whispered. Everybody's on pins and needles, wondering what you're going to tell the school on *The PB and J Report*!

"Yeah," said Armin. "And why are you keeping it from us? You tell us everything!"

Micah wasn't sure how to handle this without lying and without making them feel left out. "I can't talk about it," said Micah. "But you'll know everything that I know really soon."

"Is it awesome or terrible?" asked Armin.

Micah looked at him strangely. "That's a weird question."

"I have a theory that all secrets are either awesome or terrible," said Armin. "Otherwise, why would anyone keep it secret?"

Lydia nodded. "That actually makes sense. So, which is it, Micah?"

"Um . . . mostly awesome, I guess. Unless you're Tre."

Tre glanced back at Micah. He looked terrified. So far, everything was going according to plan. PB and J had given him a note to get him out of class for the big announcement. They didn't know what it was yet, but he'd promised them it was huge. Micah walked up to Mr. Turtell's desk, handed him the note, then headed out the door. It was go time.

Micah could relax, knowing he was doing the right thing.

So, go ahead and relax, he thought. *Starting . . . now . . .*

Why couldn't he relax? As he walked to PB & J's studio by the office, Micah wondered what was wrong with him. Why was his brain acting all weird? Making him feel bad about something that made so much sense?

Was it possible he was doing the wrong thing? That seemed unlikely. After all, he'd thought this through. Micah went over his reasoning again: (1) Revealing Tre's secret would push Tre away from his friends, setting Micah's life back to normal; (2) everyone would know that Micah had been right about Tre the whole time; and (3) revealing people's secrets was a constitutional amendment . . . or something like that. Yep, he was looking at it from every angle.

Except maybe one: Tre's. What did it look like from Tre's angle? If he were Tre, what would he want?

Rats.

The more he thought about it, the more Micah realized he and Tre were more alike than he thought. Micah could remember a few times when he had tried to be someone he wasn't. Tre, like Micah, had talents and abilities—there was no denying Tre was a great actor, even if he wasn't on TV shows or in movies. But he also struggled to fit in and find his place . . . just like Micah.

Micah could relate to Tre pretending to be someone else. Micah's dad was always telling him to be comfortable in his own skin, which sounded weird and a little lame. But maybe he was right! He needed to be happy being who he was, and that meant also accepting others for who they are and not getting jealous of them or comparing himself to them. Micah was Micah and Tre was Tre and there was plenty of room in Middletown for both of them.

But now he'd come to the end of the road. There in front of him stood the glass walls of the recording studio, with PB and J seated within.

What, exactly, was Micah going to do now? He had no idea.

He walked into the recording studio. The show's theme song was just beginning, broadcasting live throughout the entire building. It was catchy—there was no denying that—but it certainly wasn't helping Micah concentrate. What was his plan? He'd better come up with something fast.

"This is *The PB and J Report*, broadcasting live from New Leaf studio!" said J.

"And we've got a very exciting announcement this morning!" said PB.

"Micah Murphy, welcome to the program!" said J.

The Biggest Stories PB and J
Had Ever Broken

- Mr. Drury's middle name is Clarence.

- The mystery meat in the lunchroom is 92 percent albino raccoon.

- Local meteorologist Stormy McAllister was once sued for plagiarizing a weather report.

- Mayor Kim's recent "family emergency" was getting himself stuck in his daughter's Princess Party Playhouse.

- PB once caught Manny from Manny's Pizzeria eating at Jack's Pizza Palace.

"Thanks for having me, PB and J," said Micah, trying to sound relaxed.

PB smiled and nodded at Micah. "Micah told us he has a huge announcement to make! I wonder what it is, J!"

"He told us it's about Tre, the star of the movie Micah's making! My guess is Tre just landed a huge role in a major movie, PB! Probably starring alongside a huge box office star!"

"Wow! That would be terrific, J! Or maybe he decided to join a hot new boy band, like the Dreem Doodz! We've all heard his awesome voice in music class!"

"Or better yet, PB, maybe Tre will announce that the whole time he's been at New Leaf Elementary, he's been secretly filming a reality TV show!"

"Wow! That would be awesome! You'd be great on a reality TV show, J!"

"You too, PB! So, which is it, Micah? What are you going to announce today?"

"Well, . . . " Micah started. He was starting to

sweat. "Actually, none of these things. It's sort of about Tre, but sort of not. The announcement is . . ." Micah paused, trying to come up with something fast. Then a light came on, and he nearly puked out the words, "We finally have a title for our movie!"

"Oh," said PB and J at the same time. This was the first thing they'd said that didn't need an exclamation mark.

J glared at Micah, clearly not pleased. "So . . . what is it?"

Rats. Micah forgot that he didn't actually have a title yet. Oh well. Time to come up with something quick.

He thought about Tre. He thought about trying to be content with who you are rather than always wanting to be someone else or comparing yourself to others.

"*You Be You!*" he blurted out. Yes, that was a pretty good title! He smiled. Then he had another brilliant idea. "*2!*"

"2?" asked PB.

"The full title is *You Be You 2*!"

"Why 2?"

"Because it's twice as awesome!"

PB and J did not look convinced.

But then suddenly their attention wasn't on him anymore—they were looking toward the door. Micah hadn't seen Tre approach, but now he was standing right in front of them.

"Tre?" PB and J said at the same time.

"Tell me you have something big for us!" said J.

"Actually, I do. There's a secret that . . . I kind of want to share. I wanted to let everyone know that . . ."

Micah had no idea what was going to happen next. Was Tre really going to break? Was living a pretend life too much to handle? Did he have to clear his conscience?

Tre sighed. "None of it's true."

"None of what is true?" asked PB.

"Everything about me. I was never in a TV show. I was never in a movie. I can't even surf or skateboard! And 'Tre' is short for Trestorian Ledorkenson. Buzznik is just a cool stage name my parents let me use."

PB's and J's jaws dropped. Micah had never seen them stunned into silence before.

"Actually," Tre went on, "one thing about me is true. I really was in a commercial once."

A small look of relief passed over PB and J's faces.

"But it was for toddler Tug 'ems diapers."

The look of relief on their faces disappeared.

Silence. Micah stared at Tre. Tre looked back at him. Micah smiled—but not a smile that said he was happy about how things turned out, or that he'd gotten what he wanted. No, it was a smile of friendship. A smile that said "I still like you, even though you're just a goofball like me."

And Tre smiled back.

PB and J, however, did not smile.

"How could you do this to us?" PB shouted.

"You made us look like idiots!" screamed J.

"And we hate looking like idiots!" PB boomed.

"The whole school believed in you!"

"You were a hero!"

"A legend!"

"A celebrity!!!"

Micah couldn't take much more. It was terrible seeing his friend humiliated like this. They needed a distraction of some sort. Some way to get them off track. Some way to get him and Tre out of there. But what would do the trick?

Ugh. Nothing at all came to mind.

Come on, brain! What is your deal lately?

Suddenly the room exploded with sound. A heart-stoppingly loud clanging noise that drowned out every other noise in the building.

Really? A fire drill again? Didn't they just have one the week before last?

But Micah didn't care *when* the last one was. He was just glad to have an excuse to escape! They all burst out of the sound room and rushed through the office door. Micah glanced into Mr. Drury's office and noticed him quickly putting on his coat. Maybe it was a real fire this time! Or, at the very least, not a drill the principal had planned on.

Micah, Tre, PB, and J quickly joined the river of bodies hurrying down the hall. Ah! Driftwood once again.

Micah glanced at Tre, who looked back at him with relief on his face. Then he looked over at PB and J. They glared back at Tre and Micah, still red from frustration and embarrassment.

But soon they were all bursting through the front doors into the wild, wonderful world outside. And to most of the students, this time was even better than before. The last alarm had interrupted lunch, but this one had interrupted class time!

"This is amazing!" Katie shouted.

"I can't believe this is really happening!" Makayla screamed.

"This is the greatest day of my life!" Eric yelled.

"The end is near!" shouted a kindergartner. Somehow, he'd made a poster for the occasion. How was that even possible?

Micah and Tre looked around for Armin and Lydia but didn't spot them. But there was Gabe, once again on the ground. "Seriously, people! How many times do we have to go over this? Stop, drop, and roll!"

Micah caught a glimpse of Chet with half a grin on his face. And he wasn't even in the middle of bullying anyone!

Suddenly, a thought popped into Micah's brain—an idea about what had really happened. Could his guess be right? He had to know.

He left Tre by himself for a moment and walked up to Chet. "Did you do this?"

Chet glared at him. "It depends who's asking."

"It's just me. I swear I won't say anything."

Chet looked him up and down. "Yep, it was me. This ain't no fire drill. I flipped the alarm. But if you tell anyone, I'll squash you like a bug."

Micah smiled. He was right! At last, his brain was working again!

But then he thought about the stuff his brain had been bugging him about all weekend—how it

wouldn't give him any peace about Tre. Maybe his brain had been working all along. He just hadn't been listening very well.

"So, why'd you do it?" Micah asked Chet. "To get Tre out of a jam?"

"Ha! I don't help nerds," Chet said. "But I also don't like PB and J acting like they run this school. And their interview with Tre sounded a lot like bullying—and that's my territory! If I accidentally helped a couple of nerds in the process of messing with their interview, so be it."

Micah smiled. That was good enough for him.

As Chet walked away, Micah saw him pull a tiny comb out of his pocket. He glanced from side to side, then ran it quickly through the peach fuzz on his upper lip.

Micah looked around for Tre. He was easy to spot. No one wanted to be around him, so he was all alone in a corner of the playground. All around, Micah heard laughter and the word "diaper" here and there.

But this just made Micah realize how similar he and Tre really were. Micah had always had trouble fitting in too. And just because he had great friends now, that was no reason to be selfish with them. There was room in his circle of friends for more.

But as Micah wandered toward Tre, he noticed Hanz was making his way over to him too.

Hanz beat him there and spoke to Tre first. "I am guessing zat you vere also lying about being rich?"

"Well," Tre said, "I never actually told you I was rich."

"You are no good to me!" Hanz started to leave. Then he spun around for one last word. "And ze playdate I was going to organize for our robot butlers is off too!"

He walked off.

Tre looked at Micah and shrugged.

"Don't worry," said Micah. "Being shunned by Hanz is probably the one good thing that will come out of all this."

Free at Last

Wow. I really admire Tre's courage to tell the whole school about his past. I can't believe how good it feels to have the truth out at last.

I was wrong about him. Sure, he had a secret, but deep down, underneath the shame of those toddler diapers, he's just a normal kid, like me, trying to find his place.

Tre and I aren't so different after all. Okay, I don't have his dashing smile and flip-worthy hair, but besides that, we're basically the same.

Therefore, accept each other just as Christ has accepted you so that God will be given glory.
Romans 15:7 (NLT)

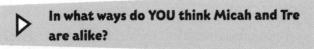

▷ In what ways do YOU think Micah and Tre are alike?

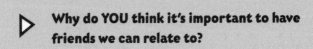

▷ Why do YOU think it's important to have friends we can relate to?

CHAPTER TWELVE

The third annual Middletown Film Festival was on the calendar for the following Saturday. And by Tuesday afternoon, the show's official program—laminated and everything—was posted on the door of the town hall auditorium. *You Be You 2* was listed on the schedule for all the world to see. True to his word, Tre had sent a rough cut of the movie to some people he knew in the business. Micah couldn't believe that he'd somehow gotten it into a real, live film festival!

Now Micah could concentrate. He was free and clear of his guilty conscience, and the pressure was on to get the movie done quickly. For the rest of the week, every day after school, Micah spent hours editing at his computer. It was so exciting to see the scenes come together right before his eyes.

Swords swished! Monsters attacked! Heroes rescued princesses! Princesses rescued heroes! Magical creatures did magical things (while showing subtle similarities to a certain floppy-eared mutt with the most range of any animal actor in moviemaking history!).

Just like the world's greatest painters—men like Picasso, Rembrandt, and Bob Ross—carefully used colors on a palette, Micah was using all the great new editing techniques he'd been learning. He was creating a masterpiece!

Or was he? It was so hard to tell if it was any good, since he was doing it all on his own. He loved being in charge of this part of the process, but he also wondered if he was completely nuts. Maybe the decisions he was making were all wrong. Maybe he was destroying all his friends' hard work. This might just be the worst movie ever made.

On the other hand, it might be the best.

But when he stopped and thought about it, both options seemed unlikely. Of all the movies in the world, being the absolute best or absolute worst was a long shot. So, he might as well do the best he could and make a movie that he, at the very least, would want to watch.

Is that what artists do? Do they just make stuff they like and hope a few other people like it too? That sounded like something he could shoot for.

So, that's what he did. And by the time Saturday rolled around, he didn't know if he'd made something that was any good, but he had definitely made something he loved.

Lydia was all dressed up, with Armin right beside her. They greeted Micah and his family at the auditorium doors. "So, is it any good?" she asked.

Micah smiled. He was nervous, but excited. "I have absolutely no idea."

Armin was confused.

"You watched it while you were editing it, right?"

"No, he edited it with his eyes closed," said Audrey sarcastically.

Suddenly Gabe popped up beside Micah. "I watch movies with my eyes closed all the time! Especially when there's a scary part and my mom covers my eyes with her hands and starts singing the Elmo theme song at the top of her lungs so I can't hear what's happening."

Audrey rolled her eyes. "That sounds awesome."

"Let's find some seats," said Micah's dad. Lydia's parents and Armin's parents had saved seats for Micah's family, so they were perfectly placed in the center of the auditorium. After sitting down, Micah watched as people filled up the rows all around them. Friends. Strangers. Children. Grown-ups. Micah wasn't expecting this many people. He knew the film festival was popular—one of the most popular events on the Middletown arts scene every year— but for some reason he didn't expect *You Be You 2* to draw much of a crowd.

As the opening theme music began, Micah settled in for the show. But for some reason he couldn't focus on the screen. He just kept watching everyone else watching the show. Right now, the crowd's reactions were all he cared about. As he looked from row to row, his eyes passed over a familiar patch of hair that bounced just perfectly when its owner moved his head. He took a second look. Yes indeed, it was Tre Buzznik hair.

Tre sat several rows in front of Micah, and beside him was a grown-up man and a grown-up woman who had "Buzznik" written all over them. Micah had never seen Tre's parents before, but Tre's dad looked vaguely familiar from behind.

The theme music ended, and the movie's opening scene began. The first monster appeared on screen. All around him, Micah watched jaws drop. That was great, right? Or was it? Was the audience frightened? Or were they just unable to believe how terrible the monster looked? He glanced back at Tre and his parents, and they seemed shocked. But in a good way?

Then, when the film's first funny lines were spoken, he heard laughter all around him. He was thrilled! But then nervous. Did they really think it was funny? Or did they think it was so preposterous they were laughing at how bad it was? What was happening in their heads?

Ugh! Why was he so insecure?!? He'd heard that was the plight of every great artist. So that was a good sign, right? But it was probably also the plight of every *bad* artist. So, no help there.

The scenes passed one after another, and Micah's eyes drifted from person to person. He watched his parents and his sister, Armin and his family, and Lydia and hers. But for some reason he spent most of his time watching Tre. Why did he care so much what *he* thought?

Micah sighed. Yep, he had to face the truth—for better or worse, he wanted to impress Tre because he respected his opinion about movies.

The minutes passed quickly as the scenes rolled on. And to Micah's surprise, throughout the entire film—all seventeen minutes of it—the crowd was shockingly silent, paying attention the whole time. They just stared at the screen, watching the world he'd created unfold before them.

Micah let out a deep breath of relief when the closing song began and the credits rolled. A Murphy Buzznik Production. It was over. For better or worse, the public had seen what he and his friends had made. And then, to his shock, the audience clapped! Micah looked from face to face, doing his best to detect any traces of sarcasm. But there were none to be seen. They actually liked it!

Everyone stood up to leave, and Micah was immediately surrounded by his friends and family.

"They loved it!" said Lydia.

"Because it was terrific," Armin agreed.

Micah's mom rubbed his shoulder. "You did a great job, honey!"

"You really did, Micah," said Lydia. "You made me look amazing!"

"You made me look heroic!" said Armin.

"You made me look hideous," said Audrey, with no expression at all. "Which was awesome."

Micah stared at his sister. It looked like she really meant this, but it was so hard to tell with her.

Two Buzzniks, along with Gabe and his mom, had now joined them, everyone introducing themselves to everyone they didn't already know.

"You kids really did an amazing job on this," Tre's mom said. "I can't believe how hard you all must have worked!"

"They really put in a lot of hours," Micah's mom agreed. "And, Tre, you were so helpful! Thanks for coming in at the last minute with all your acting and sword-fighting skills. You looked great on screen!"

"I was okay, but Micah fixed a lot of it in editing." Tre smiled at him.

"So, Gabe," Micah's dad said, "how'd they get you to look so deformed?"

"First, I was wearing my Thomas the Train backpack under my cloak," Gabe announced proudly. "Second, Lydia did great makeup work on me. And third, the squirrel attack roughed me up good, adding a lot of nice cuts and bruises!"

Micah's dad raised his eyebrows but didn't ask any questions. His dad was good like that.

Tre's dad walked up and put his arm around his son's shoulder. "Well done, kids," he said.

Micah slowly looked up, knowing he'd heard that voice somewhere before.

"Tre, it looks like you've found a great group of friends here in Middletown."

Micah's jaw dropped to the floor.

Maxx Dryver?! Could it be? Was Tre's dad Micah's all-time favorite TV cop? Micah couldn't tell at first without his stage makeup and police uniform. But that deep voice was unmistakable.

Micah looked over at his friend with eyes wide and mouth still agape.

"Shhhh," Tre whispered, lifting a finger subtly to his lips. "It will be our little secret."

The next afternoon, Micah, Armin, Lydia, and Gabe met Tre downtown to celebrate their success. They decided it was time to introduce him to a Middletown favorite. An iconic establishment. A proud monument to great taste and local flavor.

SmoothieTown!

Micah walked from the counter to the booth, holding a tray of five, gigantic orange slimes. He hadn't even bothered to ask his friends what they wanted. Orange slime was *the* drink of the New Leaf fifth-grade crowd—a refreshing blend of peaches, yams, and ranch dressing.

At the booth, everyone was chatting away about how awesome the night before had been. Lydia was looking at an actual newspaper, made from paper and everything. "The *New York Times* declares, '*You Be You 2* is an absolute triumph!'"

"Did the *New York Times* really say that?" Micah asked.

"No," said Lydia, holding it up for Micah to see. It was just the local paper. "Surprisingly, the *New York*

Times does not cover our local film scene. But the *Middletown Daily* said *You Be You 2* was 'surprisingly watchable!'"

"That's awesome!" said Gabe. "I love watchable movies!"

Micah had to agree. That's all he'd really been aiming for anyway.

"I can't believe you're only going to be in Middletown for a few more months," Micah blurted out before thinking. Everyone put down their smoothies in shock.

"What?!" Lydia asked. "Since when? You just moved here." She looked crushed.

"Yeah, Tre. What does Micah mean?" Armin added.

Tre looked at Micah. Micah looked at Tre and mouthed a silent, "Sorry, dude."

After a few awkward seconds, Tre spoke up. "It's true. The plan was always to stay here in Middletown for six months while my dad filmed a movie."

"A movie?" Armin asked. "You said your dad was

in the business, but I didn't know he was a movie star."

"He's not," Micah said. "But he is a TV star." Micah looked at Tre to make sure it was okay for him to share their big secret. Tre nodded, and Micah continued.

"You know my all-time favorite TV cop, Maxx Dryver?"

"I guess so," Lydia answered. "You know I don't watch much TV."

"Well, *I* know Maxx Dryver," Armin exclaimed. He paused for a moment, and Micah could see his brain connecting all the dots. "You've got to be kidding me?! I knew I'd heard that voice somewhere before!"

After the big reveal, the friends sat and chatted about life in LA, being the son of a big star, and what it was like to move to a new town, knowing you'll be leaving again soon.

"It's been tough," Tre shared. "I was glad for the fresh start because although my dad's gig has gained him lots of popularity, my own five minutes of fame sort of ruined things for me."

"I can't imagine what you've been going through," Lydia said. She still had stars in her eyes when she looked at Tre. A half-decade-old diaper commercial wasn't enough to change her mind about this guy.

"I never thought I would find good friends. Especially friends that accept the real me, diaper jingles and all."

Everyone laughed, but the mood turned serious pretty quickly.

"I'm just sad I have to leave in a few months," Tre said.

"Let's not think about that just yet," Micah answered. "We could film another movie before you head back to LA!" He raised his camera in excitement.

They all liked the sound of that.

Tre picked up his smoothie, and Micah quickly got his camera into position. He didn't want to miss a shot of Maxx Dryver's son drinking a SmoothieTown orange slime for the first time.

"Okay, so this is the taste sensation that everyone's been talking about, huh?" Tre asked.

"Yep," said Armin. "I'd sip it slowly at first. It takes some getting used to. You're a rookie, after all."

But Tre ignored him. He looked around the table, meeting everyone's eyes, lifted the cup to his lips, and chugged it down in one long swallow. Then he slammed the empty cup back down on the table and wiped a drip of slime off his lips with the back of his sleeve.

"That was awesome!" Micah shouted, his camera rolling so he could catch what would inevitably follow.

Tre smiled proudly, dimples flashing for all the world to see.

Then, without warning, the dimples disappeared.

His eyes got wide, eyebrows lifting to the ceiling.

His cheeks went from pink to pale to green.

His mouth opened, like he was about to scream.

Micah knew what would happen next. Orange

slime would shoot out of Tre's mouth like a T-shirt cannon, then splash all over the floor at his feet.

But then, to his amazement, it didn't! Tre actually kept it down. Nobody had ever kept down orange slime on the first try!

Or even the second. In fact, most Middletown kids drank a good fifteen to twenty of them before being able to train their bodies to suppress the natural urge to upchuck the disgusting beverage.

Tre, it turned out, was one of a kind.

Micah, Armin, Lydia, and Gabe looked at traded glances and smiled. Then they looked at Tre.

Micah nodded. "Look out, YouTube. Tre is back, and better than ever!"

You Be You, Too

Tre did a lot to hide who he really was. I mean, I would too if I was the baby in a diaper commercial. But his facade had me missing who he really is . . . a good friend.

It's ironic that I thought Tre and I couldn't be more opposite but it turns out he's more like me than I thought. (Except for the fact that Tre's dad is Maxx Dryver! How cool is that?!)

I tell you what: being skeptical is exhausting (especially in the middle of making my first "full-length" film), but I learned a few lessons . . .

IT'S NOT HELPFUL TO COMPARE YOURSELF TO OTHERS.

We all have different gifts and talents. Just because other kids are better than me at . . . whatever . . . doesn't mean they're a threat. There's more than enough room on God's great earth and in His plan for all of us! When we waste our time with jealousy and comparison, we miss out on all He has for us.

GOD MADE YOU, SO YOU CAN BE CONFIDENT BEING YOU!

God doesn't make mistakes. He knew exactly what He was doing when He made you (and me)!

So, we can be confident being ourselves, and we can be kind and celebrate those who have different strengths.

Now that I'm past all the jealousy and we're great friends, I've learned something super important from Tre. His Cali vibe may have been an act, but the kid sure does know how to be chill. I definitely need more chill in my life.

Pay careful attention to your own work, for then you will get the satisfaction of a job well done, and you won't need to compare yourself to anyone else.
Galatians 6:4 (NLT)

▷ **Do YOU ever struggle with comparing yourself to others? How does it make you feel?**

▷ **What's your favorite thing about being YOU?**

MR. DRURY

PRINCIPAL

MRS. GRITTNER

ENGLISH

MEET THE

MISS PETUNIA

DRAMA

MR. TURTELL
HISTORY

MR. BEAKER
SCIENCE

TEACHERS

MR. SPINOZA
ART

DENNIS
CUSTODIAL ARTS

About the Author

Andy McGuire has written and illustrated four children's books, including *Remy the Rhino* and *Rainy Day Games*. He has a BA in creative writing from Miami University and an MA in literature from Ohio University. Andy's writing heroes have always been the ones who make him laugh, from Roald Dahl and Louis Sachar to P. G. Wodehouse and William Goldman. Andy lives with his wife and three children in Burnsville, Minnesota.

About the Illustrator

Girish Manuel is the creator of the Micah's Super Vlog video series and a producer at Square One World Media. He lives in a little place called Winnipeg, Canada, with his lovely wife, Nikki, and furry cat, Paska. Girish enjoys running and drawing . . . but not at the same time. That would be hard. He tried it once and got ink all over his shoes.

Have you ever felt like you couldn't do anything right?

We all do stuff that we shouldn't do.
Maybe we've told a lie, or even stolen something...
When we go our own way instead of God's, it's called **SIN**.
Sin keeps us from being close to God
and it has some other serious consequences...

but I've got some good news!

GOD LOVES YOU!

°Yes, the amazing, **incredible,** Creator who made the universe **and everything in it** (including YOU) **loves you!**

How do I know this?

Because God is my friend. And He wants to be your friend too!

Check this out:

When we sin, the payment is death (Romans 6:23). But God gives us the gift of eternal life (John 3:16). That's because of what Jesus did for us on the cross.

What did Jesus do exactly?

Jesus, God's very own Son, came down to earth to save us from our sin and restore our relationship with God! He did that by living a perfect life (without sin!) and taking the punishment for OUR sins when He was nailed to a cross (a punishment for really bad criminals back then)!

Jesus did this because He loved us enough to take OUR punishment! But that's not the end of the story. Three days after His death, Jesus rose from the grave, proving that God has power over sin and death!

So, what now?

Even though there's countless things we have done wrong, God can forgive our sins ... no matter how many or how big they are! He wants to have a relationship with you through Jesus!

Check this out:

Everyone sins (Romans 3:23). No one measures up to God's glory. But God's free gift of grace makes us right with Him. Jesus paid the price to set us free!

How?

Even though we can't do anything to save ourselves from sin, we can be saved because of what Jesus has already done! By trusting Him with your life, you can live free from guilt and shame, knowing that YOU ARE LOVED!

If you're ready to accept God's gift and live LOVED, simply pray this prayer:

Dear Jesus, thank You for loving me and dying on the cross for my sins. Today I accept God's gift of salvation and I invite You to be the King of my heart. Please forgive me of my sins and guide me as I grow in friendship with You. Jesus, I want to be more like You and share Your love with others. Thank You that I don't have to be perfect but can grow in faith as I follow Your ways. In Your name I pray, amen

WORDSEARCH!

```
N H H A Z F C S J P A M U S T A C H E
X P O W H Z J I E P V H F D D S U Q L
L A F G K E H E N X B J J W L N A V C
H W T A F M L W G A L D M H C S L B O
M W S F H M X O P Q H A F H C V A W K
W L X G H E L R T Y J D B Q J H C X S
H B F C O M M E R C I A L J K Y T G N
A H F F Q O E F T Y C I O P H X A V M
L U H F D S A X B K M B V C U U T S H
P A N C V N R J A L X I M N G E E Y O
F H A T D S F H U W B C B O E G R W Y
R P V F R Y I T U P A K U C M Y T M U
I V M E J H W H Z L L L K S S W O R D
E F G E L A O R W I U K X N D M T P T
N P A O C H Z D U S E H V E B E S L S
D Y P T R E V T I L D G U I W D B N A
H P F C O N F I D E N T I A L Q P S H
```

Hug Ems
Tre
Aunt Rhodie
Sword
Hunchback
Fry It Up
Mustache
Friend
Commercial
Confidential
Tater Tots
Helo